Lock Down Publications and Ca$h Presents

THE RUTHLESS LIFE

FILLING BODIES IN THE DIRT

Written By

TOMMY COOK

First Edition 2025

Printed in the United States of America

Lock Down Publications
P.O. Box 944
Stockbridge, GA 30281
www.lockdownpublications.com

Like our page on Facebook: Lock Down Publications
www.facebook.com/lockdownpublications.ldp

Stay Connected with Us!

Text **LOCKDOWN** to 22828 to stay up-to-date with new releases, sneak peaks, contests and more…

Like our page on Facebook:
Lock Down Publications

Join Lock Down Publications/The New Era Reading Group

Visit our website:
www.lockdownpublications.com

Follow us on Instagram:
Lock Down Publications

Email Us: We want to hear from you!

Acknowledgments

To God, the best father in the world, for his patience and his love. To my mother, the best mother, Jeannie Cook, for her patience and motivation. To my beautiful wife, Roseanna Nicole, for her patience as well. And the love she gives a thug with a broken heart. She helps me repair it daily. To my editor, for his vision, editorial advice, and steady hand with words. To everyone at Lock Down Publication, especially CA$H, for his tireless work on behalf of this book trying to help bring it to some enjoyable for the people needing a little entertainment. To Kevin Gates whose music sustained me through long days of writing. To my five kids, Jeremiah, Tommy Jr, Jamiyah, Kamiyah, and Maleah. And not to mention my two step kids, Jeresi and Kourtney. To my cousins, Ken, Calvin, Anthony, Dwright, Tony, and Jimmy Downing and Jimmy Sims, and my siblings, especially my sister, Nicole. Aunts, uncles and the ones that locked up behind bars. Free my nigga Brandon Cooks, Miguel Gutierrez, Stanley Wiley, Michael Queen, Darrel Nervis-Peters and Charquevya Burns-Kirkendal.

Chapter 1

The Most Evil Son of a Bitch in the World

"Oh fuck, oh fuck!" was all Lil' D heard as his babymama got her pussy pounded by Ruthless. He had been waiting for Lil' D's free one-minute phone call from the county jail, and what a perfect time.

"Say, Lil' mama, yo' phone going off," Ruthless told her, slamming into her hard.

"It . . . ain't . . . nobody . . . It . . . can . . . wait," she moaned, just above a whisper.

Ruthless started to pound her pussy even harder. When he saw her eyes roll back into her head from the intense pounding she was receiving from his 11-inch dick, he reached over and grabbed her iPhone and pushed the talk button.

"This is a collect call from the Dallas County Jail." Having been in the county jail numerous times, Ruthless pressed the #5 button on the keypad and quickly rested it back where it was.

"Oh my God! Oh my God! I'm 'bout to squirt. I'm about to squirt again. Ohhhhh myyyyy Goddddd!"

"Hello? What the fuck! Hellooooo!" Lil' D yelled through the receiver.

"Ooooooh fuccckkk, daddy! Right theeeerrreee!" she screamed, but couldn't hear her babydaddy because of the loud screaming she was doing. Little did she know, it would soon be over. Ruthless pulled out a big Glock from behind his waist and pressed it to the side of her face, and pulled the trigger. Her head exploded; the point-blank shot damn-near tore her head in two.

BOOM! BOOM!

“What the fuck was that! Brittany! Brittany!” Lil’ D screamed through the phone. Blood and brain matter splashed all over the bed and sheets. Ruthless wiped the blood from his face, and picked up the phone, and said, “Brittany is no longer with us.”

“Man, who the fuck is this?”

“Yo’ worse nightmare.”

“Look, I got $250 thousand dollars in my safe—”

Ruthless, cut him off. “Yeah, I know it’s already in my duffle bag.”

“What? How? Hold up, man! What is this about? Where is my son?”

“Oh, he’s about to be dead in a minute.”

“I swear if you touch my son, I will kill you!”

Ruthless laughed! “You can’t kill what you can’t touch.” Ruthless walked over and picked up the nine-month-old baby out of the crib. He was crying but soon stopped once Ruthless held him close. “It’s going to be alright, lil’ man.”

“Please, man, I’ll do whatever you ask, please don’t hurt my boy!”

“Too late.”

Snap! The room erupted with loud crying.

“Noooooo!” Lil’ D screamed.

“Goodbye.”

“Lil’ D heard the phone operator loud and clear. He couldn’t think of a person that would hurt a nine-month-old baby. He dropped to his knees and cried like his baby boy.

After Ruthless broke the little baby boy’s arm, he laid him back into his baby crib and walked out into the living room where he picked up his ringing phone. It was his boss, Cash Indigo, the biggest boss from Jamaica.

“You got my money?”

"As promised," Ruthless said through clenched teeth as he picked up the bloody duffle bag filled with nothing but Benjamins.

"Meet me at the mansion in fifteen minutes."

"Remember, you once told me never shit where you sleep."

"You right. Meet me downtown under the bridge next to the Hooters at 7 p.m."

"Bet, that's perfect timing for me." Ruthless gathered his things, wiped down all evidence, picked up the duffle bag, and walked out of the room. On his way out of the condo, he stopped and stared at a large photograph. In the frame was a man with his wife and newborn baby. His name was Darius, Lil' D, Smith. He was a small-time hustler from Moneyhound Court in Oak Cliff.

In state jail he met a Jamaican by the name of Deng Indigo. He was the nephew of Cash Indigo a powerful, powerful man. Deng used to tell Lil' D all these big money stories of how he got this and how he did that. He even told him about how ruthless his uncle's *Voodoo Mafia* crew was. They were known for half the deaths in Jamaica, now they were killing shit in Dallas and in Houston. They were even more dangerous than before.

Ruthless stared at the picture with disgust. He opened his mouth and spit a mouthful of spit directly in Lil' D's face. He didn't know why his boss would deal with a lowlife like him, but like every other murder he'd committed, it always dealt with a lowlife who couldn't pay what they owed. If you do business with Cash Indigo and don't pay what you promised, you best believe Ruthless was coming at any given time. He was Indigo's main shoota, and his name spoke for itself. He had well over 22 bodies to his credit, and his murder count was still rising.

Before walking out of Lil' D's condo, he painted 23 in blood on the front door and disappeared down the hall.

An hour later, Ruthless pulled up to a gated community that sat right next to a lake the size of an ocean. All he could think about was the dead presidents inside the duffle bag that sat in his lap. It was $250 thousand dollars in cash sitting inside the Goyard bag that his boss thought was being delivered to him in a short while, but Ruthless had something special for Mr. Indigo.

He planted his white Air Force Ones on the pavement and climbed out the whip. On his way towards the crib, he stopped and gazed at his pretty white bitch that stood on all fours in front of him. He rubbed his hand across the side of her smooth body. He loved her to death. She had a price tag of $300,000. She was right off the showroom floor. Her name was Lamborghini Aventador.

A lot came with killing: a life sentence if caught, probably even the death penalty, but riches came with it too. And over the years, he received a lot of bloody payments. He had no respect for the dead. But he loved fast cars, clothes, bad bitches, and jewelry.

He bent down and wiped the white Forgiato rim. He just loved that car. When he looked up, he saw all the other beautiful luxury cars he had lined up in his circular driveway. He blew a kiss at his all white-on-white Rolls-Royce Wraith. She was also a beauty. Mostly all his cars were white, for it symbolized the seven years he did in TDCJ, after just serving four years in the Jamaican military. The same military that turned his body into a weapon. He could kill you in the blink of an eye.

He turned his head when an SUV came creeping up his driveway. He reached for his glizzy, but if he wanted the person dead, they would've already been greeting the angels in Heaven. He knew exactly who was in the pink G-Wagon.

"Ruthless, I didn't know you was out here. Where the money you wanted me to run through the money machine?" Jucci asked as she walked out of the big-ass house, walking towards him.

Jucci was a beautiful Cuban bitch with measurements that would shut any Kite DM magazine model down. Her measurements were 34DDD-28-44, all natural. She walked towards the whip, red thong peeking out of the ass-hugging jeans she wore with a designer tank top. She had her jet-black curls laid down her back at the tip of her 44-inch ass. She grabbed the bag and made her way back inside the house, not before looking back at the man she grew to love. Their eyes locked for a moment. They had a bond like no other. Just looking into her eyes had him going crazy. Her eyes were innocent, but those same eyes had seen a lot of death. She had killed a lot of men with those same eyes, literally. She too was a cold-blooded killer, and a lot of men had died under her spell. Ruthless called her the Black Widow; once someone was in her web, they were dead.

Ruthless' mind traveled back to a time when they did their second kill together.

Throwback ...

SQUEAK! SQEAK! SQUEAK!

Lil' Vic was breathing loudly as he tried to keep up with the Cuban bitch, her 44-inch-wide ass making it hard for him to focus. She threw that ass back like a professional. Her fat ass moved like water. Nobody's ass could bounce the way Jucci's did. Lil' Vic was lost, staring at her swole ass, so lost he didn't hear Ruthless creep up behind him.

"Oh, shit, I'm about to cum," he roared.

"Nooo! You're about to die!" Ruthless announced, pressing the .357 to the back of his skull.

Lil' Vic's body got so stiff he stopped pumping into the Cuban bitch's wide frame. He was surprised to see the Cuban's ass still bouncing. She was still throwing it back on him while a gun was pressed to the back of his head. Then it hit him.

"You grimy ass bitch!" was the last thing he ever said before half his head got knocked off.

BOOM!

"Damn! You couldn't wait until I got my nut off? Fuck!" Jucci vented, still throwing it back on a lifeless Lil' Vic. "Hold up, ooohhh fuck! Ohhh fuck! I'm cumming! I'm cumming, aahhhhh!"

Several seconds later, Ruthless watched her walk towards the restroom.

"I'll be out in a minute. His wall safe is already opened. I'm not gone keep putting you on like this." She winked at him.

Ruthless smiled at the fine Cuban bitch, who later became part of his hit squad. He trained her and four others in everything the Jamaican military had taught him.

After taking a quick shower, Jucci walked into Lil' Vic's living room, butt-ass naked. Just before, she had been covered in blood, sweat, and nut. Now, she was dripping wet, with a towel wrapped around her head. Ruthless was stacking dead presidents into the two duffle bags.

"So, I'm in with you and Voodoo Mafia?"

"No, you with me. You part of me now, and I trust you with my life. I hope it's the same on yo' end too."

"It is, I promise." She smiled, and after that bloody day, they created a bond like no other.

Present Day . . .

Ruthless watched as the SUV's doors popped open, and out came four beautiful women— all thick and ex-strippers turned into vicious killers. The driver's name was Bugatti. She used to be an adult film star and stripper. She was popular on Instagram, OnlyFans, Twitter, and TikTok. She was a tall, thick bitch standing 5'6" with a lot of ass and titties. She had tattoos all over her body. She was dark as fuck. Ruthless examined her from top to bottom. Her bombshell body was out of this world, with measurements 34DDD-28-48. Nothing but ass sat under the designer dress she rocked, and it moved like water.

She passed him with a frown on her face.

"Hmmpf," she spat out. "Why you called for an emergency meeting when we all stay under one roof? You couldn't wait until we all got back home? I mean, I do got other shit to do instead of hearing yo' bullshit about robbing yo' boss," Bugatti vented.

"Yeah, I don't understand that either," the high exotic-looking bitch said, pulling down her dress over her juicy ass. She was the prettiest out of the four women, but Bugatti had her beat in the ass department. Corvette's measurements were 32DD-25-42. She looked Ruthless up and down with a mug on her face. She was Puerto Rican and Black. She looked like Instagram model @iamashleemonroe.

"So, all you hoes feel like that?" he asked, looking at the youngest of the group. She was only 19, but she was the deadliest after Ruthless. She was high yellow, with measurements of 34-27-39. She was smaller, much smaller than her foes, but she was born a killer. She once stabbed a man 11 times before cutting his dick off and shoving it down his throat for trying to play her in a club she used to dance at, right before she met Ruthless and he changed her life and pocketbook.

"Hoes! Boy, you got me fucked up!" Lexus vented through clenched teeth. She was the second-youngest of the four women. She was 20 and had a sassy mouth, with measurements of 32-26-43. She patted her Glock that was tucked in her waistband. The jeans she wore looked painted on her thick thighs and wide hips. She was a big booty redbone. She looked like Instagram model Alexis Sky.

"Chill out, Lexus!" Mercedes said.

"Mercedes, I'm not about to kiss his ass like you do, real talk."

"Bitch, whatever!" Mercedes spat.

"Y'all both need to shut the fuck up!" Bugatti shouted. "We will be inside," she announced, sashaying inside the $600,000 house.

Ruthless looked at all five ladies he'd turned into vicious killers and shook his head. They each had a unique story of how he met them, and how they became a part of him.

Jucci unzipped the duffel bag and poured out stacks of bills onto the circular glass table, then ran the money through a money machine, not once but twice. The total came to $252,368.00.

"It's a little over $250 thousand."

A smile spread across Ruthless' face, flashing his VVS that beamed like the sun. "Now, we split it down evenly. $41 racks apiece."

"What about Cash?" Bugatti asked.

"What about him?" he spat.

"Ain't that his money?"

"Fuck Cash. He will be dead in a little while."

"Oh, really?"

"Yeah, all I need for y'all to do is stick to the plan I been going over with y'all for weeks now."

"So, you serious this time?" Jucci asked.

"Yeah!" Ruthless answered as he pulled his designer shirt over his head, revealing a ripped body that was completely tatted. He had tats everywhere— face, neck, chest, stomach, back, legs, and thighs.

"You do know not only the Voodoo Mafia will be after you, but the Dominican Diamond Cartel as well."

The Dominican Cartel was run by Angel Rantiello Jr. He was full Dominican, so was everyone else inside the multimillion-dollar drug operation. His father ran the cartel like his father before him. But that all ended when he had a son with Cash Indigo's daughter. That broke their Dominican bloodline, being that her father is full Jamaican, or should I say Black, giving his son mixed blood. To be the head of the Dominican Cartel, you had to be 100% Dominican.

"Fuck the Dominican Cartel. I have the best killers you can buy standing behind me."

"Hmmm!" Lexus spat.

"Well, everyone but one," he joked.

"Boy, shut the fuck up. You know I got yo' back no matter how much you get on my nerves."

Ruthless knew Lexus was telling the truth. She'd proven herself to him many times before. He thought back to his recent stare-down with death. He was locked up in a Hilton Hotel presidential suite downtown, blowing on some Sour Diesel with a big booty Mexican stripper he met at XTC 2.0. Ruthless hit the blunt hard and long and mean-mugged it. It was that gas. He looked down in his lap. Mia was giving him the best head of his life. Her head was doing a fool between his legs.

SLURP! SLURP! SLURP!

He had to admit she was a fool. A straight headhunter. "Damn, ma, turn up then."

In the lobby, four Mexican men stood outside the door of Ruthless' room, all armed. Just when they were about to kick the door in, Lexus came out of the room next to the Presidential Suite, wiggling in her tight-fitting jeans. She locked eyes with the four clowns. All four of them did very poorly at trying to conceal their automatic weapons. Before any of them could blink, Lexus charged at them, catching them all off guard. She kicked the first one in the face. He dropped his gun, which she caught with ease. She slammed the gun down on the second man's knee, snapping it and causing him to shoot a wild bullet that hit the third man in the eye, sending him crashing to the floor. She brought the gun back up and slammed it in the fourth man's face, knocking teeth out of his mouth. She then fired a shot at the first man just when he made it back to his feet, shooting him point-blank in the head.

She then turned her attention to the second man; he was on the floor in pain, holding his cracked knee, rocking back and forth.

When Ruthless heard the shot right outside his room, he snatched up his Glock and ran to the door. He looked back at Mia. She was trembling all over. She had her iPhone in her hand, texting away. Before Ruthless walked out of the room, he already knew what it was. What Mia didn't realize was he was with that type of shit. He lurked in the shadow of strip clubs trying to find a weak nigga with money, stunting like he was Birdman or Floyd Mayweather. He had five beautiful bitches willing to do anything for him. And all five beautiful bitches were trained to kill.

Then he would attack, taking everything — money, guns, dope, and jewelry. Then they'd leave.

As soon as he stepped into the hall, he saw Lexus standing over four Mexican men who were armed. Three were dead; one was still breathing.

"Hold up."

Ruthless punched the man in his knee, then went through his pockets and pulled out his iPhone. He remembered the men from the club — how could he not remember the patent-leather green Gators the Mexican men wore? Lucky for the Mexican men, he didn't have a PIN code programmed to his phone.

Ruthless went straight to his messages and saw he had just received a new text message. It was from Mia, the same bitch that sat in the Presidential Suite with nut running down the side of her face.

He read the message and quickly became enraged.

Text: *Papi, is you alright? I didn't know this black fuck would have someone watching us. I swear I didn't. Please, Papi, are you okay?*

He clenched his teeth and went to her earlier messages.

Earlier Text: *Papi, I got this black fuck throwing money up in here like he just hit the lotto. He supposed to be leaving with me later. You want to get at this dumb ass nigga?*

Reply: *Of course. I just made it to the club. I'm outside getting ready to come in. Go to the Hilton Hotel — this* *should go smoothly. The black shit will never see it coming. Make sure you suck him good. I hope you still been watching Victoria Cakez.*

Ruthless had seen enough. He turned his gun to the Mexican man, and at the same time he and Lexus let the man have it.

BOC! BOC! BOC! BLOCKA! BLOCKA! BLOCKA!

Once they riddled the man up, they both walked inside. Mia's eyes widened as they fell upon her. Ruthless pulled the trigger, blowing her lower jaw and teeth out of her mouth. Blood burst from her damaged face, pouring down the front of her bare chest. She was coughing up blood, choking and trying desperately to breathe. Ruthless and Lexus showed her no mercy. They aimed their guns and let her have it at the same damn time.

BLOCKA! BLOCKA! BLOCKA! BOC!

Her body twitched from side to side. Lexus and Ruthless made eye contact as both their guns went the fuck off. They probably didn't see eye to eye at times, but they both loved to kill. They smiled at each other while Mia was long gone to the afterlife.

Ruthless smiled at the memory. He later asked Lexus how she knew it was gon' play out like that. Her exact words were, "She brought me on a lick before back when I used to dance at XTC. The men we killed were her baby daddy and his uncles. Once I saw you leave with her, I knew what it was."

After that day, she earned his trust.

"So, you really want to do this, Phinehas?" Mercedes asked.

"Yeah, load up the choppas, we 'bout to make it rain blood in Dallas."

Chapter 2

Five Bad Ruthless Bitches

Bugatti stepped into her room that was located on the upper level of the house. She peeled off her dress and walked towards the edge of the bed. She pulled back the silk sheets and examined each Glock laying on top of her queen size bed wrapped in chrome.

The sight of her Glocks made her pussy wet instantly. She picked up the chrome-plated .44 and kissed the side of it. "Brrrrat!" she yelled, admiring it as if it was a twelve-inch dildo.

"Is you ready to go?" Ruthless asked as he appeared in the doorway.

"Let me ask you some. Why you wanna bite the hand that feed you?"

Ruthless screwed up his face. "Bitch! I help him eat! Get that shit right. If it wasn't for me, Voodoo Mafia wouldn't been shit, and Angel and his Dominican Cartel would've taken over the drug trade in Dallas"

"I'm just asking. Damn, calm down."

"I know this might be hard to deal with and all that Cash dick won't no longer be in yo' mouth, but he's dead and whoever stand with him," Ruthless whispered in her ear while wrapping his arms around her naked body from behind.

"First, fuck Cash. His dick ain't never been in my mouth. I'm just looking out for me and the others because you are sure not. It's only about you and that bitch Benny," she snapped with pure disgust rolling off her tongue.

Benny was Ruthless' only weakness, and she was also his biggest threat. She was Cash Indigo's only daughter, and he loved her more than anything. Like most powerful men, they always spoiled their little princesses. When it came to Benny, she got whatever and whenever, while her baby brother had to prove himself to their father. Ben was a killer, but he wasn't a ruthless killer. He was more in it for fame than fortune.

Ruthless yanked Bugatti around and grabbed her roughly by the chin. "Bitch, don't never bring that bitch name up around me. Do you understand?"

"Damn! Let go of me. You are hurting me!"

"Do you understand me?"

"Yeah, damn!" She pushed his hand away and walked towards the full-length mirror to examine herself to make sure she didn't have any bruises. She stared at herself for a second before she felt Ruthless' hands all over her body. She loved when he lost his temper, then turned around and kissed her ass. "I swear you're bipolar as fuck!" she said as she turned and faced him. He put a finger over her lips, then leaned over and kissed her—lightly at first, then harder. She grabbed the back of his head and pulled him closer. He sucked her lips into his mouth, then her tongue.

He continued to kiss her for a while before venturing lower, planting soft, wet kisses on every inch of her neck. She shivered a bit, and pulled back, but he drew toward her again.

Seeing her big tits and hard nipples, he couldn't help but to bury his between her tits, inhaling her floral scent.

He flicked the tip of his tongue over one of her nipples, then tongued round and round the areola. She moaned audibly. The lust in her eyes told him she wasn't disappointed.

He led her to the bed. It was inviting and sensuous, with a misty green satin sheet and fluffy down pillows.

Bugatti pulled his designer shirt over his head, then reached down, slowly unzipped his jeans, and pushed them to the floor. She pushed him down on the bed. She pulled one Gucci shoe off, then the other, then pulled his jeans off. She leaned down and began crawling up the bed, stopping to run a hand over his calves and thighs.

His dick was hard and sticking out a bit of his Gucci briefs. She reached in and took hold of his throbbing dick. She played with it while stroking it, once in a while stopping to graze her fingertip over his balls. This drove him crazy.

She took just the tip in her mouth and circled her tongue round and round the head, stopping now to suckle the foreskin, before taking almost the whole thing in her mouth. She sucked the dick with circular hand strokes—up and down, up and down at the base of the dick. She kissed the shaft all up and down and sucked one ball after the other into her mouth.

After what seemed like forever, he had to stop her. He reached down and pulled her on top of him. She rubbed her wet pussy over his dick until she took his throbbing dick in her hand, and guided it into her pussy. She gasped and held him deep inside her, taking all his dick. She began raising and lowering her hips—up and down, up and down, so slowly that he could barely stand it.

Her big tits were bouncing slightly with her up-and-down motions, and he had a front-row seat for the show. She looked good as hell, with her head thrown back and her eyes closed, concentrating on riding the shit out of his dick. She opened her eyes, fixed them on his, and increased her tempo of the rise and fall of her hips. Her ass jumped faster and faster.

"Oh shit . . . Oh shit!" Bugatti cried out.

Ruthless took full control over her pussy, beating it like it owed him money. He was meeting her thrust for thrust. Her enormous-ass titties were dangling in his face. He captured one in his mouth. The nipple was stiff. He kissed it, he twisted the opposite nipple gently in his fingers.

He gripped her chunky ass cheeks, spreading them far apart.

"Ahhhhhhh! Fuck—this—pussy," she stuttered. He slapped her ass, and it jiggled on her back like water in a bowl.

She let out a long sigh and whispered, "Baby, we got to get to ready."

They continued fucking longer than she thought they could hold out.

"Ooooh shit!" Ruthless roared as he pounded her back in. He thrust one final time and blasted a stream of cum in her.

They both sank down on the bed among those soft green sheets and lay panting for a long while. Ruthless was drained. Bugatti eased herself off his chest onto the bed and curled up beside him. She reached down to caress his still-swollen dick, looked over at him, and said something every nigga needed to hear. "Baby, that was the best dick ever. I will do whatever you tell me, I swear."

"Go clean yourself up and meet me at the checkpoint at seven. Don't be late."

Later…

While driving the white Mclaren 570s up interstate 35, Ruthless weaved in and out of traffic, missing cars by inches. All he could think about was murder.

As soon as he pulled up at Cash's mansion, he saw six of his bodyguards sprawled out with their heads leaking blood and their last thoughts.

The vibration on his lap drew him from the bloody scene that was before him. He picked up the iPhone 17 and read the text:

Mercedes: *It's done, bae. All six are down.*

Reply: *I know, I'm here. You did good, ma. Was it loud?*

Mercedes: *Not at all, I'm good at what I do.*

A slow evil smile crept across his mouth as satisfaction was in his cold eyes. He knew she was a damn good shooter with a sniper rifle. He taught her what he learned years ago. It took years to teach but she was gifted to kill

Ruthless parked by a line of luxury cars. He climbed out with shotgun down by his side. He walked up to the front door and rang the doorbell, ready to blast whoever answered the door. After about a minute or two, the door was snatched open. To Ruthless' surprise, it was Cash Indigo's nineteen-year-old son Ben. He was toting an AR-15.

"Wassup, nigga?" My father not here yet."

Ruthless was taken back to see him there. He usually was out with a bunch of bad bitches, spending all his of father's money on drugs and parties.

Ruthless didn't even speak; he raised the shotgun. pointing it at Ben's stomach and fired. The blast tore opened his stomach, allowing his intestines to fall free, cascading to the floor at his feet. He fired the shotgun again but at his shoulder. The force lifted him off his feet and somersaulted him through the air. He crashed down to the floor. Blood was pouring from the remains of his shoulder and stomach. He stood over him. Ben spit out a wad of bloody phlegm.

The gunshots echoed throughout the mansion. Ruthless stood over Ben's lifeless body, holding a big-ass shotgun when Zoe rounded the corner. She put her hands over her mouth. The pain she felt from the sight of the dead body didn't allow her to scream. Ben lay on the floor with his guts spilling out like spaghetti. It was gonna be a closed casket.

Ruthless looked up and noticed a pair of eyes on him. He smiled at the Jamaican beauty with that Indian mix in her blood. She wore half to nothing in a silk designer robe. Underneath the robe she was completely naked like the day she was born. She had just gotten out of the shower when she heard the gun shots. She grabbed her robe and told her two Jamaican servants to continue to work. She thought it was just her son playing with one of his many guns in the house again. She was about to let him have it until she saw a man standing over him.

Ruthless had no remorse as he smiled at Zoe. She opened her mouth to scream but Ruthless had raised the shotgun to her chest.

"I wish you would, bitch," he spat, and ordered her to lay face down on the floor next to her son in his fresh pool of blood.

"Who else in the house, bitch?"

M-my . . . t-two . . . m-maids," she stuttered above a whisper.

"Where at?"

"Upstairs. Please just kill me already."

"Where is the little boy?" Ruthless asked.

"Noooo, noooo, please don't hurt my baby. I'll give you whatever you want. I do whatever you want, please!" she cried.

Ruthless picked up the shotgun after tying Zoe's hands tight with her son's Gucci belt. When Ruthless yanked at the belt more guts spilled out of his stomach. Zoe gagged at the sight.

"Why is you doing this? Is because of what my daughter did to you?" she asked with tears flooding down her face. He didn't reply. She watched him disappear down the hall.

"Do you hear me, you son of a bitch! That's Benny's pussy. She can fuck whoever she wants. You were fucking over her anyways!" Zoe yelled after him.

Ruthless crept upstairs toting the shotgun. At the top he saw two Jamaican women. They had to be servants because of the outfits they wore. Both women trembled at the sight of him. He quickly ordered both of them to lay face down on the floor. He looked around, trying to find something to tie their hands together with, unsuccessfully. He looked down the backs of the two thick women and let his eyes settle on the one on the left, her ass standing out the most. He had to admit she had a fat-ass booty. But he was there for their souls not to lust at no maids.

"Nooo!" the Jamaican woman screamed when she felt him yank her skirt up. He then yanked her panties down and right off her body, and tied her hands with the thin fabric. After tying the other woman's hands together, he went and searched in every room until he found the one-year-old little boy whose name was Brazil. The baby was dark with a head full of curls. To Ruthless he looked just like his mother Benny, and not a bit like his father Angel Jr.

Ten minutes after finding the kid sound asleep, Ruthless laid the two servants down next to Zoe in the same pool of son's blood. After a minute or so, Zoe heard the clicking sounds of Ruthless' designer shoes, letting her know he was returning. She looked over at her grandson. He was sound asleep on the leather sofa. She still couldn't believe he was still asleep after all the gunshots that could be heard throughout the house. But then again, they lived in a big-ass house; the shots probably never reached where he was.

When she strained her neck to look at Ruthless, her eyes widened with fear. He carried her great-great-grandfather's Machete with a duffle bag in the other hand.

"What is you going to do with us?" she cried.

He didn't respond; he just smiled a wicked smile and gripped the machete tighter. He plunged the machete into the side of the thicker maid's neck. She coughed, spitting out blood. He pulled the knife free. Blood squirted from her lacerated arteries. Then he did the unthinkable, he lifted the machete over his head, then slammed it downward, slicing her over and over. Zoe gasped; a hand clamped to her mouth to prevent herself from showing any weakness, but the other maid screamed so loud it could've ruptured a muthafucka's ear drum. Especially when the woman's head rolled across the marble tile. The screams of both women filled the house. Ruthless took the machete and wiped it across Zoe's curvy body before slicing it swiftly across the other Jamaican girl's face, leaving a trail of blood.

"Please! My husband has been good to you . . . hell, I have been good to you. Look, my husband has $10 million in diamonds in the lower part of the basement in his vault. Please, just let me and my grandson walk out of here unharmed, please!"

He didn't reply or show any sign that he cared for the diamonds. In his eyes all she saw was hate and more hate.

"Why do you wanna do this for, Phinehas? Because Benny fucked over you?"

Ruthless laughed. "Nah, bitch, because I want yo' soul," he spat, raising the machete over his head once more.

"Noooooooooooooo!"

An hour later, Ruthless had the bodies chopped in a million pieces, stuffed into a Louis Vuitton duffle bag, and was now on his way towards the checkpoint. He lifted the blunt to his lips and exhaled hard. He blew out the exotic smoke of Strawberry Banana. And thought only of killing Cash Indigo.

7:01 p.m.

When Ruthless pulled up, the first thing he saw was Cash's two bodyguards standing on each side of the black-on-black Maybach. He pulled alongside the Maybach. Cash had the curtain pulled back like the boss he was. Inside, Ruthless could see a huge-titty white bitch's head bobbing up and down in his lap as he pulled hard on a Cuban cigar with his head tilted back.

Ruthless reached for the moneybag and retrieved it. He stepped out and walked toward the Maybach just when Cash was stepping out.

"You got my money?" Cash asked.

"As promised," Ruthless said, handing him the duffle bag.

Ruthless surveyed everything. He watched Cash's bodyguards' every movement as he watched the big-titty blonde inside the Maybach sniff a line of white powder. He watched as Cash opened the bag and saw his face instantly frown up.

"What the fuck is this!" Cash barked, grabbing at his chest.

"Boss, what is it?" Cash's bodyguard said, reaching for his Glock.

"Hold up, he's having a heart attack!" the other bodyguard yelled, running toward his boss. He caught him in his arms just before he crashed to the ground.

"What the fuck was in that bag, Woo?" Abu yelled over his shoulder.

"Nigga, I don't fucking know!"

"Look and see. Fuck! He doesn't have a pulse!"

Woo turned to ask Ruthless what was going on, but he was already gone.

"Where did Ruthless go?"

"Fuck him. We will catch up with him later. See if the money in the bag," Abu yelled, trembling all over.

Woo walked over and picked up the bag. He peeped inside and yelled, "The fuck!" He threw the bag, causing it to flip over near Abu. He had to swallow hard to keep from throwing up when Zoe's head rolled across the pavement. Inside the bag were pieces and pieces of Cash's entire family.

"Say, man, where did the white bitch go? She was just here!" Woo asked.

"What do you mean?" Abu asked as he slowly laid Cash's body down on the pavement.

He walked over to the Maybach, and sure enough, the big-titty blonde was gone.

As soon as Abu got in front of the Maybach, his whole head exploded.

"Gotcha," Mercedes said as she put another round in the sniper rifle and let that bitch go.

Before Woo could react and process his next reaction, a bullet went through his head as well.

"Bang! Bang!" Mercedes shouted.

Back at the Crib…

Ruthless looked at the four beautiful women that sat in front of him. He loved Bugatti. She was amazing to him. He loved Lexus's aggressiveness; she was down for whatever. He loved Corvette — she was about stacking her munyun just like him. He loved Jucci; like, literally he loved her. They shared more than the other women shared. She was with him longer than any of them.

Mercedes walked in through the double doors with the big-titty white girl close behind — the same white girl that set Cash Indigo up. His eyes lay on Mercedes; she was his number five. He loved her the most. She reminded him of himself: hungry for blood and willing to kill anybody to be on top.

"Ladies, it's our time now. It's time to lock down the city. Let me introduce y'all to our newest member — her name is Bambi." He looked each woman in the eye before he said, "But before we can lock down the city, we must eliminate our enemies."

Chapter 3

Voodoo Mafia

Benny stormed outside, surrounded by four of her father's men toting Uzis and TEC-9s.

"You tripping, ma, for nothing," a tall Dominican with a long ponytail said.

"This is not like my mother. She always answers the fuckin' phone. My daddy and brother are not answering. I can feel something not right, Angel," Benny said. She was mixed, and being mixed with so much shit she was the prettiest bitch in the world to whoever looked upon her. She was 5'1", 130 pounds. Her measurements were 36-27-45. Then, on top of that, she was so tatted she could've put Lil Wayne to shame. She could've literally been the cover girl for *Urban Ink* Magazine.

She wore a white designer wife-beater with some black spandex tights that made her ass cheeks look as if they were suffocating.

"Your father might've took them all out to a fancy restaurant. Call the house and ask the maids or guards."

"I did, Angel, and they're not answering. I got a bad feeling in the pit of my stomach."

"Man, fuck!" Angel turned to his men that stood behind him and spoke some shit in Spanish. Whatever he said, they rushed off and came back strapped for war.

"Let's ride out!" Benny told her father's men. She walked over to the black-on-black Range Rover, throwing that big ass of hers in every direction. She climbed in once all her men were inside and burned off with Angel and his Dominican Diamond Cartel following right behind, three cars deep.

As soon as they pulled up to the big-ass mansion, Benny's heart dropped to her stomach. All her daddy's top bodyguards lay dead around the mansion, leaking blood and brains.

She jumped out of the Range Rover with her four armed men right behind her, guns in hand. Her eyes widened with fear when she saw that the door was slightly ajar. Her heart was pumping at a rapid speed. She didn't want to believe that her entire family was dead. She couldn't.

Benny crept up to the door, pushed it open, and pointed her gun left to right, looking for any reason to blast her twin .45s. When she walked deeper into the house, she had to turn her head quickly from the sight. In the middle of the marble floor was a pool of so much blood it looked as if a group of people had died right there. But instead, it was two women, both with their heads cut off. Both heads were a short distance away from the owners' bodies.

Benny felt like all the air in her lungs left her.

Once Angel and his men arrived, they couldn't believe what they had walked into. It looked like a war zone. Blood was in every room, like the killer was just walking room to room.

"There's nobody here, but it's blood all over the house, Benny . . . more blood than it is right here," the big black Jamaican announced. He was Cash's most loyal soldier and not to mention his most dangerous one, too. He stood at 6'3", 210 pounds, all muscle. His name was Goldmouth. He was an ex-NFL football player that got into some real bad debt with her father. To pay it off, he killed a few muthafuckas for the family and soon became head of security.

"Goldmouth, where is my son?" Benny shouted. She didn't care about the blood. She wanted to make sure it didn't belong to her son.

"He's not in the nursery room or either of the other rooms."

At that moment, both parents hurried off. Benny looked in one room while Angel looked in all the others. When they returned, all their men were standing around looking sad and confused.

"Who did this? Who did yo' father have beef with?" Angel asked.

Benny looked at him with a sour look. "You know with who . . . with your people. Y'all still think my father had something to do with yo' father's murder," Benny said, now aiming her guns at her baby's father, her men following suit, each side now aiming their guns at one another.

"Nah, we didn't have shit to do with this. We ended the bloodshed over a year ago between our families once you had Brazil, remember."

"And that was the same day your father died, and ever since then you and your family have been looking at mine upside down."

"Baby, you're tripping for nothing. Our baby is missing; we got to get him back."

"How is we going to get him back if he's dead?" she said, dropping to her knees.

"Baby, don't think like that. Just know we didn't have shit to do with this." Benny closed her eyes and tried to block out the image of her son somewhere slumped over. She just didn't know who would send a blackout on her entire family. Whoever it was, she promised they were going to die.

"What is this supposed to mean?" one of her men asked, staring at a bloody number on the wall.

"22," Angel whispered, even though the numbers were written on the wall in digits.

"What is that? A gang or some?"

When Benny opened her eyes, she stood and stepped towards the bloody number on the wall that read 22 big as day. She didn't know how she missed it. Her heart pounded hard. *THUMP! THUMP! THUMP!* She shook her head in disbelief. "No! No! No!" she screamed.

"What is it, baby?"

"I know who did this," she said, tears falling down her face.

"Who? Tell me who so we can go kill that son of a bitch!"

"It was Ruthless," she whispered.

Chapter 4

Cat and Mice

"We need to put aside our differences and work together," Angel told Benny.

"He-killed-our-son. We can go half on his body, but my organization is out for blood. We're going to catch him with or without you."

Angel was speechless. He didn't want to a war with a man like Ruthless. He was going to lose a lot of money and definitely a lot of men.

"I will do it alone. You know both our fathers hated each other. Your father only ended the war because I got pregnant by you. My father would never allow for these organizations to come together."

"Are you insane, Benny? You or Voodoo Mafia can go up against a man like Ruthless. He is not one of those thugs or want-to-be gangsters you killed in the past. This is a trained killer, the same man that trained you and five other women."

Angel's words hit her like a ton of bricks. She knew just how dangerous Ruthless was. Once upon a time they were the black Bonnie and Clyde. But they weren't robbing banks; they were robbing drug lords.

Back in the day…

Dressed in all black and some True Religion army-fatigue pants, Ruthless carried a military-issue M16 he took from a pawn shop. He crept through Heavy Red's house as if it was his own. Heavy Red was that nigga in the funk. He moved heavy weight, twenty-three bricks at a time, and to get this close to a nigga like him was what every hustler dreamed about.

Heavy Red was deep off in Benny. He had fucked her more times than he cared to count that day. He thought she was just another freak from the hood, not knowing she was a ruthless killer.

"Mmmm, baby, fuck this pussy."

"Damn, you a freak, bitch."

"I love this dick," Benny grabbed him and pulled him in deeper, flipping him over so she could ride his dick like a cowgirl. She sat on it sideways and began to bounce like she was on a trampoline.

"Okay, ride that dick like that then," he spat, looking at her round ass bounce up and down like a Wilson basketball. Heavy Red had to admit; Benny was the prettiest bitch he had ever seen. He knew she was mixed; she was too exotic not to be. He had really let his guard down with her, like most men did.

His dick was wet and shining with her juices as she repeatedly bounced on the dick. Her tits jiggled over his chest. He spread her ass-cheeks apart and slowly worked his finger deep into her ass. He sawed two fingers in and out of her hole. She tossed her head back. He started to hammer into her, which caused her to collapse against his chest.

"Fuuuuccck!" she moaned and did a full 360 on the dick, staring at her man. She continued to ride while Ruthless lurked in the darkness with her shotgun.

She made her ass cheeks jump on the dick like a jackrabbit. He stared at the crystal chandelier that hung above his king-size bed as her booty clapped inches from his face like hands. He was unaware of an audience, not Benny. She rode his dick while searching the soul of her true lover.

Ruthless stood there with the shotgun. She hopped off the dick quick, like she was trying to get over a hurdle. Heavy

Red was confused until he saw the man lifting a big ass shotgun directly at his chest. He was angry, his face was red, and his hands were balled into tight fists. He stared at Benny with pure hatred.

"My people gonna kill everyone y'all love."

Ruthless didn't give him a chance to say anything else. He aimed the shotgun at his legs and fired.

Heavy Red screamed as the shot tore through his knees, practically tearing his lower legs off. Blood splattered as his kneecaps exploded, the flesh shredded like raw salad.

"You know what this is. No need to be stupid. Give me the money and you keep yo' life. You play games, you die, and I will flip this bitch upside down. It really doesn't matter to me," Ruthless spat, but Heavy Red wasn't trying to hear that shit. He was still screaming. He was lying on his back, rolling from side to side, clutching his demolished knees. His left leg hung loose from his knee, his foot and ankle held in place only by the ruined, bloody tendons. His other leg was stripped to the bone; it was a mass of mangled meat.

"You fuckin' bitch!" he screamed. "I'm gonna kill you! You hear me? I'm gonna fuckin' kill you!"

"I'm gon' ask you one more time. Where is the money?"

Heavy Red gritted his teeth, trying desperately to subdue the searing agony he was in. He coughed, spitting out a ball of phlegm.

"Suck my dick!" he scoffed a laugh, groaning in serious pain.

Ruthless was done playing.

"You said suck yo' dick. How about I blow the bitch off."

He pressed the barrel of the shotgun into his groin. Heavy Red's eyes begged him not to do it, but he pulled the trigger, blowing everything off—dick and balls. The noise he made was like nothing Ruthless ever heard before, a combination of a scream and a cry for mercy. He placed the shotgun to his chest and fired once again, killing him dead and leaving a pothole in the middle of his chest.

Ruthless looked back over his shoulder, watching Benny's ass as it did flips toward the bathroom. Unfortunately, they didn't find any money, but she learned a valuable lesson. Don't fuck with Ruthless. But she was all in now. She was ready to die for her son. She needed to find Ruthless. She was going to kill him.

Two days later...

In North Dallas, Ruthless loaded up his Draco. He sat in a beat-up old Dodge Charger waiting like a lion to attack his prey. While he was caught up with murder on his mind, a red-on-red Bentley GT pulled up in front of the house he was lurking.

Out came a woman so beautiful and exotic it looked like she was from another planet. She was a deep chocolate peanut-butter brown, with skin just as smooth, and an ass so fat it looked impossible to tote. She walked up to the exotic whip and leaned her head inside. The boy shorts she wore did her ass no justice on how it was bunched up in her large ass.

Ruthless saw that the driver wasn't alone. Soon as the driver's tinted window came down, he noticed another dreaded-up nigga in the car.

Ruthless was just about to unload on the opps when he saw the chocolate bombshell spin around and yell toward the house. He watched as a duplicate of herself walked out. She was a little bit thicker with a whole lot more ass. He continued to watch as the driver's side door opened. A big Jamaican man hopped out fresh in an all-white 2828 outfit on.

"You looking good, daddy," the thicker twin said. Her name was Jakia. She wrapped her arms around Goldmouth's neck.

"You know this me every day. I got to stunt on these pussy boys." He stepped back and admired both sisters. They could have easily given the Double Dose Twins a run for their money. Both women turned with their backs to him and started to make their ass clap.

Goldmouth touched a button on his iPhone 17 and Future's voice blared out from the $100,000 whip. Both women could have started a small earthquake with all the ass they were shaking.

"I don't give a fuck if they were real sisters," Future's voice boomed.

Ruthless had seen enough. He hopped out the beat-up old Charger, gun ready to kill. If Goldmouth hadn't had both sisters twerking on him, he would've seen Ruthless approaching, gun at the ready. He moved quickly. He stepped out the dark shadows and approached the Bentley with caution. One of Goldmouth's YNs' head was facing the biggest ass he had ever seen. He never witnessed the horror that came behind him. Ruthless pressed the cold steel to the back of his head and pulled the trigger twice. The shot tore through the back of the man's head, obliterating his brain and thoughts.

"What the fuck!" the twins both screamed. They laid eyes on Ruthless and turned to run inside with Goldmouth right behind them. He turned and let loose on Ruthless.

BLOCKA! BLOCKA! BLOCKA!

Ruthless quickly ducked behind the Bentley with a sudden sense of panic rushing through his blood. He could hear the twins going in on Goldmouth. He ducked inside the house.

"What the fuck is goin' on? Somebody shot yo' nigga! Who the fuck was that?"

Ruthless got up and unloaded on the twins' crib. There were screams. He was sending tons of glass and splinters flying everywhere.

They were having a shootout in broad daylight like they were in an old western movie.

"Bring yo' bitch ass outside, bitch-made ass nigga!" Ruthless screamed.

BLOCKA! BLOCKA! BLOCKA!

Goldmouth ducked behind the wooden door just in time to prevent himself from being shredded like a sheet of paper by the shot.

"Stay right there, pussy. I got my niggas coming. We 'bout to end yo' bitch ass today!" he laughed.

Ruthless didn't find the shit funny. But he had to move. He kept his Draco pointed at the house and got somewhere. He already knew Goldmouth was gon' call for backup. After waiting for a few minutes, he saw a fleet of luxury cars pull up to the front of the two-story house. Several Jamaicans with assault rifles hopped out. He smiled when he saw Benny's exotic ass climb out one of the Range Rovers.

Each of her men searched the entire area, starting with the beat-up old Charger. To their surprise, Ruthless was nowhere to be found.

"Where is he, Goldmouth? Which way did he go?"

"I don't know, Benny, he was just out here. He ran to that—standing by that piece of shit of a car—before y'all pulled up!"

Benny looked over her shoulder back where six of her men were still inspecting the old Charger, then it hit her. It was a trap.

"Get away from the car!" Benny screamed, running toward her men.

But it was too late. The car blew up in a ball of smoke, killing everybody that was near it.

When the smoke cleared, six of her best men were killed. She couldn't believe she had played Ruthless' twisted game. He knew all along what he was going to do. He knew who the weakest in her crew. He used to be her father's most trusted shooter. He knew Goldmouth had a weakness for the twins. He knew just where to find him. Ruthless executed a plan and put the shit in motion.

Benny got enraged when she heard how Goldmouth was bragging about almost killing Ruthless. Six of her best men were dead because of him.

"Man, y'all should had seen how I had that nigga jumping from car to car like a little bitch."

"You don't get it, don't you," Benny shouted, interrupting his laughter. "If he wanted to kill you, he could had done it the moment you pulled up at Jakia and Kendra's crib, but he knew you was going to call me. He knew just where to run too. He played you and me. He played all of us."

Chapter 5

Kill Me If You Can

"Damn, that bitch got a fat ass," Ruthless heard a man shout. He turned his head just in time to watch Jakia strut by, flaunting an ass so big it was ridiculous. He smiled from ear to ear, just the bitch he was looking for. Jakia and her twin sister Kendra were, hands down, the baddest bitches in XTC 2.0. Together they made a profit close to 5 racks a nigga and were still chasing the one-hundred-dollar bills.

It had been a couple of days since the shootout in front of their house. They were still a bit shaken up, but money always came first. It wasn't hard for Ruthless to find where the Chocolate Dose Twins bust it wide open; they were the talk of the city. And ever since the shootout with Goldmouth, it had been extremely hard for him to catch any of Benny's men alone. They easily mobbed up together six to eight deep, sometimes deeper.

He sat quietly, lurking in the darkest part of the club. He wore a basic black tee, hiding behind some dark shades. He watched Jakia's every move. His plan was first to sex them both off the rip. Then lure Goldmouth and his Voodoo Mafia puppets to him. Then he was going to execute from there.

Ass jiggled and bounced all around the club, but Ruthless ignored them all. He had his eyes set on everywhere Jakia bounced that big ass. He finally spotted Kendra. She had just come out the dressing room and hopped on the main stage, where she worked the pole and her big ass. Jakia climbed up onto the stage to join her sister. Both women did what thirsty niggas came to see them do. They put on a show; they made bare ass clap like a drum set.

"Show time." Ruthless had them just where he wanted them. There were a couple of broke niggas close by the stage throwing one-dollar bills when he stepped up. He hoped they didn't remember him from the other day; hopefully the bussdown Cuban links around his neck drew their attention from reality.

Jakia and her twin instantly noticed Ruthless. He looked and smelled like money. They both were frozen into his gaze. They didn't have a clue who he was. They both started to bounce their ass cheeks that were so fat it made a sound of thunder. The DJ cut the music. All you heard was a loud clapping sound.

BOW! BOW! BOW!

Ruthless made it rain so much on the stage that it took two waitresses to shove all the money into two trash bags. The money really got the twins' asses jumping from 0 to 100 real fast.

"I like you," Jakia, the much thicker twin, said. "What's yo' name? You look familiar as hell."

He didn't reply; all he did was continue to pop rubber bands, making it shower over the club. After all, it wasn't his money. It was Benny's father's.

"So, it's like that? You are too good to tell us your name?" Kendra asked with attitude.

"When y'all done entertaining these broke niggas, come and fuck with me—a real nigga that really about that life. I'll be posted up in VIP," Ruthless spat, looking at each nigga that stood near him up and down.

"Broke!" one of them yelled, eyes burning fire into the back of Ruthless' back as he walked toward VIP with a smirk on his face. He smiled at the man's toughness, trying to put on in front of the chocolate beauties like he had balls or something. A lot of men had lost their lives trying to impress a bitch.

Meanwhile, a thick waitress helped the twins count all their money. Jakia and Kendra were stuck thinking about Ruthless. He was different from all the other niggas to venture off in the club looking for pussy and ass. They could tell he was cut from a different cloth.

"Bitch, I think we done hit the jackpot with ol' boy."

"With who, bitch? The nigga with the bling on?" Both sisters looked at each other like, "Bitch, what!"

"Bitch, don't say that nomo."

Jakia looked at Kendra and both sisters busted out laughing.

"Damn, I see y'all getting all this money in this bitch," some big-booty stripper said, noticing all the money scattered all over the place.

"Yeah, bitch, you already know how we do," Kendra boasted.

"We out this bitch. We got money to chase," Jakia said as she sashayed out the dressing room. She didn't have time to be friendly with them hating-ass hoes.

Meanwhile, Ruthless sat in V.I.P. watching the stripper who favored the Dallas rapper Erica Banks. Her fat ass bounced and jiggled provocatively.

"Damn! they bad," the twins heard as they sashayed towards V.I.P.

"Look at that ass," Jakia looked back over her shoulder as a group of YNs pointed directly at her round 48-inch ass.

Kendra grabbed her twin by the arm aggressively and pulled her. "Fuck them broke ass niggas. We need to get to this rich muthafucka before one of these thirsty ass hoes do," she spat, throwing her ass as she strutted on by.

Ruthless looked up in time to see the twin coming his way. He whispered something in the stripper's ear, and she quickly picked up her money. On her way past the twins, she mugged them both before looking back at Ruthless. He slowly pulled on the blunt he'd rolled earlier, blowing out Gelato in the air.

While Kendra danced ass naked on the table in front of him, he motioned for Jakia to turn around. She proceeded to make her huge ass cheeks bounce all around him. Ruthless popped band after band, flooding the twins with one-hundred-dollar bills. He was trying to win them over.

When Jakia faced him with naked titties bouncing in his face right near his mouth, he heard "Ahhww, shit." He saw Goldmouth and about eight Jamaicans enter the club. He smiled from ear to ear as he watched Jakia's massive ass cheeks jump. He knew some shit was about to unfold. Jakia ignored his presence and kept making that ass clap in Ruthless' face. Kendra, on the other hand, was scared shitless. She knew one of them hating-ass hoes was gon' rat her out. They were gon' have more dirt than necessary.

"Bitch, what we gon' do? These hating-ass hoes gon' tell Goldmouth we been with this nigga all night," Kendra whispered.

"Fuck them hoes and Goldmouth. He knows we're dancers, the fuck!" Diamond shot back.

"You know he's going to be mad when he sees us over here dancing for another nigga. Remember what he did last time."

"Bitch, he is not about to shoot this bitch up again. Stop worrying so damn much and get this munyun."

"That's y'all nigga or some?" Ruthless asked.

"Some like that," Kendra said, staring at Goldmouth. He had shut down the picture booth. They were taken pictures by the dozen with hoes, bottles, and a bunch of money. He demanded respect, and Ruthless could see the fear in the twins' eyes as they watched him like a hawk.

"Meet me out back. We can finish this party at my house as long as the money keep coming," Kendra said.

"That's a bet. I'm ready to go anyway. I hope buddy don't pop up at y'all shit on no crazy shit."

"Hell naw. He got our shit shot up a couple of days ago. We done moved on his stupid ass," Jakia said before giving Ruthless a small kiss on the lips. She wanted him bad. She felt secure in his presence.

A short while later, Goldmouth sat quietly on the wall until he saw Jakia and Kendra. The twins came from the VIP area wearing nothing at all. Their meaty asses caused every Voodoo Mafia member to look.

"The fuck y'all been?" he barked at them with hate in his eyes. "Y'all didn't' see me standing here?"

"Naw. We just emptied this fuck nigga's pockets. We missed you tho, daddy," Jakia hissed wrapping her arms around his wide frame.

Outside the club, Ruthless had snuck out the back. His plan was executing just like he'd expected. A few minutes after, he sat low in his McLauren and watched as both twins walked out the club's back door, then he honked his horn. When they came over, they inspected the foreign whip from inside out. It was white and fast. And most definitely expensive.

"How is all of this going to fit in there?" Jakia joked, pointing at her sister's big ass.

"I'm going to meet y'all back at y'all spot. Send me the addy. I got to handle sum shit real quick."

"You better come spend some more money with us."

After a few hours, Ruthless switched cars and clothes. He had instructed the girls about the play and was now on his way towards the twins' house. He reread the text from Jakia:

Bigbutt Jakia: Make a right on Highlands and go straight down, then make a left on Hunnicut. I stay in the first house on the right.

When Ruthless pulled up in front of the twins' house, he climbed out the Audi R8 and proceeded up the steps. He knocked on the front door, and a second later the door was snatched open by Jakia. She stood their ass naked and oiled the fuck up.

"I see you serious about yo' paper."

She didn't even let Ruthless step all the way in. She pushed him to the wall, dropped down to her knees, ripped his pants open, and slowly engulfed his dick in her mouth—every last inch. She looked at him with her dark brown eyes as her warm, wet lips kissed their way up and down the shaft of his dick. She tickled it with the tack in her pierced tongue. And went to work, taking the dick so deep inside her mouth that her chin bumped against his balls. He heard her fingering her wet pussy, and her lips made slurping sounds as his dick slid in and out of her mouth.

"Bitch, I swear you ain't shit. What you trying to do, cuff all the dick for yourself!" Kendra cried out. She stepped up wearing a tight white tank top that showed an abundance of cleavage that was cut just over her juicy 34s. She was naked from the waist down, pussy lips fat and ready.

"Fuck you, hoe, nobody 'bout to wait on you." Jakia rolled her eyes, rubbing Ruthless' dick all over her face and lips. "You want it faster, daddy?" She pulled back a little. He grabbed a handful of her hair in each of his hands like they were pigtails, and then fucked her mouth with just the head of his dick.

"Come here, daddy, let's go over to the couch where my sister is complaining about me not sharing the dick." He helped her up and watched as she walked over and sat on her sister's lap.

"Daddy, come over here. I swear you'll love my sister's big ass tits. They're pretty amazing," Jakia admitted and blatantly looked down her shirt.

Kendra looked at Ruthless and then back at her sister, sizing up the situation. Jakia smiled at him, then carefully cupped both of her sister's large titties in her hands and winked at him. "They're so fucking big." She gave them a jiggle. Kendra blushed. Jakia started to caress one of the nipples. Both of women looked at him.

"I bet you want to do this." Jakia buried her face between her sister's magnificent tits and shook her face between the flesh. "Come eat this pussy, daddy." She spread her legs on her sister's lap. Ruthless pulled up a chair and began sucking on her pussy. She moaned and screamed like a porn star as he licked her pussy like a cat would some milk.

"Take yo' shirt off!" Jakia told her sister, and she did as she was told. Ruthless stopped to watch as Kendra big tits fell out of her tank top. She leaned over so her nipples dangled in her sister's mouth. She caught them hoes in her mouth as Ruthless started back sucking on her clit.

Jakia screamed and moaned so loud that he knew the neighbors heard.

Her legs were twitching and squirming, and he could tell she was about to cum. He licked her clit faster. She screamed louder, and her body tightened. When she couldn't hold it any longer, she busted all her juices all over his face.

"Oh, nigga, that shit was fucking amazing," Jakia said. "Let's go to the bedroom so he can fuck us."

They hurried to the bedroom, and Jakia had Ruthless sit on his back so she could ride his dick. Kendra also climbed on top of him, but she sat down on his face. He began sucking her clit while reaching up and squeezing those big ass titties.

Jakia was sliding slowly up and down on the dick. She reached over and fingered her sister's pussy while he licked it.

"Oh, give me another one," Kendra begged Jakia.

She slid another finger in, and then another. Kendra bucked and bounced on his face in the same rhythm that Jakia was riding his dick. Kendra's pussy was getting very wet; he was making slurping noise as he sucked it.

"Kendra, get Binky from out the dresser." Kendra hopped off his face and pulled open the drawer on the nightstand and produced a strap-on dildo and a bottle of lube. She rolled off him and squirted a wad of lube on his dick, then guided him slowly into her ass. Damn, she was tight. He reached around and grabbed her tits while he fucked her in the ass. Her sister fed her the dildo slowly and plowed that big dick inside her. He looked over Jakia's shoulder as she rode the dick and got fucked in her pussy at the same damn time. He watched as Kendra's big tits jiggled from the force of the pounding and the aggressive look on her face as she fucked her sister.

Ruthless fucked her faster, trying to match the pace of Kendra, who was fucking like a beast.

"Oh, fuck, you guys are going to make me scream," Jakia said, her big ass making a clapping sound as Ruthless pounded away, and he heard Kendra smashing into her pussy.

"Oh, shit! Oh, shit!" Jakia yelled as her body convulsed with wave after wave of pleasure. Ruthless grabbed her small waist with both hands and went dumb. *WHAM! WHAM! WHAM! WHAM!*

"Ooohhh, shit!" Jakia screamed as she released all her juices on his dick.

Afterwards, both sisters left Ruthless and went to shower together. That gave him time to go to the car. He grabbed his shotgun and came back through the crib slowly. They were still showering when he walked into the bathroom. They had a built-in frameless glass shower, where you could see right in, but the steam didn't allow them to see danger lurking behind the barrel of a shotgun. He snatched open the door. Jakia screamed and outstretched her hand trying to grab him. Ruthless raised the shotgun and fired. The shot tore through her hand, leaving them hoes looking like shredded confetti. He shot again, hitting her in the shoulder. Blood oozed from the holes in her body. All Kendra could do was scream until he took aim, pointing the shotgun at her head. The shot took her head clean off her shoulders. The remains of her head hung loose from her neck as blood poured from the stump, flooding the shower floor.

After wiping the blood and gore off himself, he went through the twins' phone and hit up Goldmouth with a bunch of lies about missing him and wanting to love on him. So of course he was down. They'd moved to a new location, so he felt safe and out of Ruthless's reach. But Ruthless was always two steps ahead.

A short while later, Goldmouth exited the Range Rover with two Jamaicans close behind him, all toting Dracos. Goldmouth glanced all around the entire scene, looking for anything unusual, but saw nothing.

Ruthless knew he had his puppet, but first he had to get rid of the Jamaicans.

Chapter 6

45s and Mac 11s

Inside the twins' house Goldmouth crept in the shadows with his Mac-11, and two shooters on his heel. "Split up," he whispered to his team. Goldmouth received a text message from Kendra's phone about coming over to have a good time, but he had to make sho she wasn't on no slime shit.

"Say, Goldmouth, I got some over here in the kitchen," Friendly Flip announced. Friendly Flip was a foot soldier in the Voodoo Mafia. He was what you called a **Hot Head**. He was always on the front line ready to spin on whoever whenever.

When Goldmouth entered the kitchen, Friendly Flip held up a note that read, "If you find us, we'll do anything you want."

He snatched the note out of Flip's hand and crumpled it up. "The twins ain't played hide and seek with a nigga in a minute. The last time they did, I find them hoes in short school skirts wit' nothing underneath. They lil' hoes wild." He smiled at the memory and told his men to make themselves comfortable. He got excited thinking about what he was going to do to them both.

When Goldmouth checked the bedroom, the twins were both underneath the silk sheets, ass naked, laying on their stomachs.

"Man, I know these bitches ain't sleep," he mumbled, looking at the time on his bussdown Rollie. It was a little after midnight when he received Kendra's text. It was now 2:35 in the morning. He laid the Mac-11 down on the counter, unzipped his pants, and walked over to the head of the bed. When he pulled back the silk sheets, his eyes expanded. Bugatti and Jucci laid there butt ass naked with Glocks pointed directly at him.

"Shhh, if you make a sound, yo' brains gon' be hanging out on the other side of yo' head, big boy," Bugatti spat. She stood with the gun still pointing at his round head.

She escorted him to the living room. Jucci stood behind him with the .45 and Mac-11 aimed at his back.

"All you muthafuckas get y'all bitch asses on the floor!" Bugatti yelled, pressing the Fo-Fo to the back of Goldmouth's head.

Friendly Flip and his associate aimed their weapons at Goldmouth, who already had his hands up in the air, and said, "Just do what they say. Put y'all guns down now."

They quickly did what was instructed.

"Get their guns," Bugatti told Jucci. Friendly Flip almost choked staring at Bugatti's 51-inch ass that poked out like a hippopotamus.

Both women stood over them butt ass naked. Bugatti made the call to Ruthless. "It's good. Come on!"

After Ruthless hung up the phone, he exited the bloody house, then jogged across the street back to the twins' house. It was too late for any neighbors to be out; he moved quietly up the steps. By the time he reached the twins' house, Bugatti was standing there with all three men, with a Glock in one hand and her iPhone 17 in the other.

Jucci patted each of them down, retrieving guns, jewelry, and wads of money. When they saw Ruthless, all three men had terrified looks written on their faces and were shaking so much it could've had stripper poles in front of them.

Ruthless locked eyes with Goldmouth. He was the only one that showed no fear. He accepted his fate. He walked up to Jucci naked ass and said, "Go get dressed, ma, you did good."

Ruthless was covered in blood, his face crimson. His shotgun was also covered in blood. He placed the barrel of the shotgun to the back of Friendly Flip's neck, right at the base of his skull. He felt him flinch away, no doubt knowing just what it was.

"J . . . just do it al . . . already. Pull the fucking trigger," Friendly Flip muttered.

Ruthless did just that. He pulled the trigger. The shot tore through his neck, shattering the back of his head like glass. His head was now loose from his body. Blood squirted where the back of his head had been. His blood splattered all over Goldmouth and Sammy Gee.

"Which one of you muthafuckas wanna die next?"

They didn't utter a word.

"I'ma let my bitch kill you." Ruthless turned to Jucci and told her to go get that machete out the car. She smiled and walked out of the house. When she returned, it was up there. She straddled Sammy Gee's back. He tried to struggle, but his hands were tied behind his back. His death was quick. She slammed the machete into his neck over and over, so many times she lost count. His blood leaked out of his body, flooding the floor underneath him.

Goldmouth laughed. He knew he was about to die. Might as well laugh death in the face. He was staring up at Ruthless. He aimed the shotgun at his head and pulled the trigger. The blast ripped his head open like he was opening up a bag. The only thing that remained was the bottom half — a nose and a mouth.

Chapter 7

Reminiscing

Benny woke up in bed butt-ass naked as usual. She opened her eyes and didn't see her other half lying next to her. She looked between her legs and saw the wet puddle. She thought she had another wet dream, but her pussy was soaking wet. She opened her legs and began playing with her pussy, rubbing it in circles. She finger-fucked herself for a while before she creamed all over her finger.

She put her wet fingers in her mouth and started sucking off the juices. She was too horny.

"Damn, where this nigga at?" she asked herself as she hopped out of bed and grabbed the blunt off the counter that was already rolled up. She walked towards the full-length mirror. She stood there with a fat and a pretty pussy. She knew she had ass for days. She blew out clouds of smoke and stared at herself. She was tatted the fuck up; her entire body was covered in ink.

When Ruthless stepped into the room, Benny was positioned sideways, all her thickness and all her juicy ass were on full display.

"Damn, you a bad bitch," he said as he came behind and wrapped his arms around her tiny waist. His hands slid down and cuffed her super soft ass that felt like two fluffy-ass pillows.

He looked down at her pierced nipples for a moment. She had her nipples and pussy pierced. When he looked back into her green eyes, she licked her succulent lips. Her tongue ring rolled across her upper lip. She pulled hard on the weed while lost in Ruthless' cold eyes. She loved them so much.

"Who told you to smoke my shit, ma?" he asked.

"Because I do what I want. I run shit here," she said seductively as she blew a cloud of Gelato in his face. She pulled hard again on the weed, then squatted in a perfect squat position in front of him. His throbbing dick began to be released from his Gucci briefs. She released his eleven inches of hard dick and blew out over the head. She began slapping his big dick across her face, gliding the head back and forth across her lips. She opened her mouth, eager to suck his dick down her throat. She started sucking and deep-throating the whole thing. She spit on it some more, then slurped it up like spaghetti. She loved sucking dick; it was always her favorite meal of the day. She put her hands on the back of his thighs and looked up at him while he rammed his dick down her throat. Her mouth was full of eleven inches of meat. She opened her mouth as wide as she could and sucked hard and fast. She shook her head from left to right. She loved hearing his rapid breathing and his lustful groans. He put a foot on the bed and fucked her mouth like it was a pussy until she gagged and choked.

After she got filled up, she crawled seductively with an ass plug between her pumpkin-size ass. She had his undivided attention. She made her ass clap nonstop. Her fat ass sounded like a stampede.

CLAP! CLAP! CLAP!

"Come get dis pussy, daddy!" Benny hissed, looking over her shoulder. She spread her huge fat cheeks apart and slowly pulled out the butt plug that was round at the tip. It popped out her tight asshole and made a popping sound. *POP!*

She dug it back in her ass and fucked herself with it, while Ruthless sat back and watched as it disappeared and reappeared over and over. After a while, he was ready to fuck some. He got behind as he held his dick with his right hand. He pushed the tip inside.

"Oh God!" she cried as he invaded her pussy. He was deep inside of her. She felt like she was giving birth.

"Yeah, bitch, take all this dick!" He started to slam back and forth inside her.

"Oh, fuck!" She pushed her hands against his chest, trying to prevent him from going too hard. His dick was stretching her pussy in ways she never felt before. He slammed in her with no regard. She talked shit to him, calling him ugly and a gorilla while he grunted like a dog.

"Fuck me harder, you ugly muthafucka!"

He glared at her and grabbed her by the neck and slammed her back into his vicious thrust. Her fat ass bounced with each stroke. He was fucking her into submission.

After a while, Ruthless slipped out of her pussy and smacked her hard on the ass and watched it wave and jiggle.

"Stop playing and put it back in," Benny begged. When he did what was told of him, she took full control. She grabbed the dick with no hands, all pussy. She threw it back on it and began working the dick like a full-time job. She bounced back, throwing all that pussy on him hard. Her ass met skin.

SMACK! SMACK! SMACK!

Ruthless could feel his nut rising. After a short while, he released all in her virgin pussy.

"Don't give nobody this dick. And I promise to never give anybody this pussy. You were my first and last. I swear on my life," Benny said as she threw it back on his limp dick like she had something to prove. She pumped all the cum into her body.

"Benny, do you hear me talking to you?" the old wise man asked as he interrupted her memory of her first love. She was reminiscing. How could Ruthless do this to her? They shared a bond like no other. Benny looked around and had forgotten that she was seated in a Chinese restaurant with a powerful man who was once close to her father.

"I'm sorry, what were you saying?" she asked the old head.

"Why do you have beef with Phineas?"

"He bit the hand that fed him. He killed my family and took my son," Benny replied with venom in each word. "He's a problem, Black Knowledge. I need your help to get rid of him. He killed my most trusted bodyguard. You might know him by Goldmouth. He was my daddy's second, and deadliest killa after me."

"Yeah, I have heard the streets talking. He even killed two famous Instagram models."

"Yeah, they were sisters, and he also killed a family next door. That's where he hid and set my men up. I need yo' help. He is a danger for business. Think of the money we're both losing. Do it for your friend, my father."

"What about Angel?"

"What about him?" Benny asked. "He offered to help, but I don't need his assistance. He will just be in my way."

"When are you going to tell him?"

"Tell him what!"

"Don't be stupid, my dear. It's going to get really ugly for you before it gets better. You're going to have to tell Angel that Brazil is not his son, and when you do, another war will begin."

Benny knew her father's old friend was right. She wanted to tell Angel from the beginning but never did because of her loyalty to her father. "My father knew I didn't want to sleep with the enemy, but the Dominican Diamond cartel was too powerful for my father. They were killing his from all angles," she said to Black Knowledge, opening herself up, something she never did before. "Why would he even want his princess to sleep with the enemy's son and then lie and tell him that my three-week-old baby was his? I don't understand that. Can you enlighten me?"

"Your father was a very smart man. He knew Angel Sr. would end the war and you did too, that's why you agreed to it. But your father is dead, and one man is killing all of yours. Now just think what the Dominican Cartel would do to you once they find out that nasty truth. You need to tell Angel first before I can assist you. You are a smart girl, Benny, do what you were trained to do. Kill your enemies."

She sighed heavily, knowing the old wise man was right. She had to tell Angel their baby wasn't his. She vowed right there in that fancy Chinese restaurant she would handle her business by killing Ruthless, the man she once loved and gave her all to.

"Remember, Benny, you must think like the killer. That's why Ruthless is always ahead on the chessboard. If anybody knows him, it's you."

Chapter 8

Game Over

Benny was done letting her guard down. She called in twenty of her father's best men.

"The bullshit is over with. I have too much to give up now. I want Ruthless dead! We have lost too many men at the hands of one man. Game time is over; everybody moves with caution."

She looked around her father's warehouse. She saw that she held every man's attention, even the two brothers, Peewee and Stacy. They were a gift from Black Knowledge. They were his two main shooters. They both were deadly as fuck. Benny looked up at Peewee. He was hands down the same size as **André the Giant**. He stood 6'6", 202 pounds solid. He was as good with his hands as he was with a gun. He was bald with a full beard. He looked like the rapper **Rick Ross** to her. Stacy was the youngest. He was just as big, standing 6'4", 196 pounds solid. He was caramel and looked like his big brother. He had a scar under his nose. He looked rough and thuggish.

"Let's move out," she said, grabbing her guns.

As soon as they stepped outside the warehouse, Benny's men dropped like flies.

THUD! THUD! THUD! THUD!

"Take cover!" Peewee yelled, shielding Benny as he led her back into the warehouse.

"Man, who the fuck was that?" Stacy asked, dragging in one of Benny's men who had a fist-sized hole in the middle of his chest.

"Drive! Drive!" Mercedes yelled from the trunk of the car. Lexus put foot to pedal and drove off, leaving a trail of white smoke.

SKRRRRR!

Ruthless had Mercedes and Lexus tail Benny from sunup to sundown. He had his Mexican partner he met in prison insert a hole in the middle of the trunk where the keyhole was supposed to be. They waited for the best opportunity, and when Benny stepped out with her men close on her heels, she knew it was do or never.

The sniper hit four of Benny's men, dropping them dead before they even hit the ground.

***

Bugatti's turn…

Finding C-Mac was turning out to be easier than Bugatti had imagined. He was slouched out on a couch in VIP with a team of dreaded up men, popping bands, and popping bottles. He was high and a little drunk. **Zillionaire Doe's 'This month' banged** out the speakers.

Bugatti had set up a lot of men, and she didn't think C-Mac would be any different. What man didn't love a fat ass and pretty face?

She looked over at Jucci. She had just walked back in the VIP area where C-Mac was seated among some ruthless Jamaicans.

"Show time!" Bugatti said.

Jucci wore a black and white, skin-tight one-piece that clung to her every curve. She loved pretending to be a stripper. She felt like Diamond off *Player's Club*. C-Mac was the main player in Voodoo Mafia's drug underworld. He oversaw one of Voodoo Mafia's most profitable drug warehouses. Benny assigned a bunch of shooters to assist him everywhere he went, and most of the time it was at his favorite strip club, DG's, where he could see his favorite two strippers, Bugatti and Jucci. He had no idea they were his enemies. All he knew was that they had fat-ass booties.

Jucci stepped in and sat right on his lap. She wrapped her arms around his neck and leaned in for a kiss on his cheek. “Did you miss me?”

He frowned and said, “What you think? It took you long enough to bring yo’ ass to me. Where’s Ocean?”

“She should be coming back out soon.” Jucci searched into his eyes and knew he had to die tonight. He was a tall, skinny nigga with full sleeves and a head full of dreads. He wasn’t no threat to Ruthless, but Ruthless wanted to rain blood on his enemies, and everyone associated with them. He knew the Jamaicans and the Dominicans wanted blood for his recent actions, so he was gon’ kill them before they could get to him.

C-Mac continued to stare at Jucci. She was a beautiful woman with an ass that would put Cardi B to shame. “Go get her. I want to make it rain on the both of ya.” She kissed him on the cheek again and rose from his lap. Her big ass was sitting in the air like a spaceship. He couldn’t do nothing but shake his head. She walked away, with both cheeks jiggling like crazy. She looked over her shoulder and counted four Jamaicans that stood in their way.

When Jucci walked up on Bugatti, she was near the bar in her G-string that was pulled up snugly into her crotch, showing off the plump lips of her pussy. Her body was thick, and she didn’t have no stomach. Deep down, she knew what Jucci was about to tell her. That C-Mac wanted her. All men did.

“He wants us to pop some pussy, right?” Bugatti beat her to the punch.

“Yeah.”

"I'm so sick of this nigga. Let me see, it's time for us to kill this nigga." She led and Jucci followed, with an eyeball full of her ass bouncing around. Her long black hair framed her pretty face and curled softly down her back in a neat ponytail. Niggas' eyes devoured her deliciously rounded ass cheeks as she walked by them.

"There go my girls," C-Mac said as Jucci returned with Bugatti and sat down beside him. As Bugatti did, her G-string pulled up tighter in her crotch, parting the lips of her pussy even more. All eyes were on them. Niggas were drooling.

"Let's get this party started," Bugatti said, and all his niggas started to squeal and yell and throw money into the air.

"Hell yeah," C-Mac said and smiled. Bugatti bent over and made her ass clap in his face. Jucci joined her, and the Jamaicans went wild. C-Mac started to smack both of their asses softly. Jucci started to dance with the four Jamaicans, and they started to throw money all over the club.

"Oh shit," C-Mac yelled. His dick was so hard he had to adjust it through his *2828* jeans before—"Damn!" C-Mac said, looking at Bugatti's huge ass cheeks clap together inches from his face. He couldn't take it anymore and buried his face between her massive ass and licked her tight asshole until she shook uncontrollably.

"Boy, you nasty. Save that for later," Bugatti hissed, bumping his face away with her hips.

"Damn, I can't help it."

"You need to try," she said as she sat on his lap and peeked at the tattoos down his *2828* graphic shirt. She grabbed hold of one of his bussdown Cuban links and pulled him close to her. She kissed him passionately as he ran his palm up and down her thick thighs. He reached around and massaged her pussy through her thin fabric. He rubbed her clit in circles. She squirmed in his lap, moving back and forth.

Meanwhile, Jucci was bent all the way over, with her ass bouncing up and down. She was smothering one of the Jamaicans with her big-ass booty. His nose was buried deep between her crack.

Corvette was dropped in a squat position with nothing on but a pink and white shoestring thong. She popped her ass like a hydraulic lift, throwing her ass everywhere but off. Bugatti was happy Corvette made it; she needed to duck off and hit Ruthless up. She finally got C-Mac to agree to be alone with her and Jucci. She continued to watch Corvette's big ass jump, one cheek at a time, before rubbing C-Mac's chest all the way down to his groin area. "I'll be back, daddy, I got to check on some."

"You leaving with a nigga still, right?"

She nodded and walked off, throwing ass in every direction. She ducked off into the locker room and pulled out a burner phone from her *Birkin* bag. It was an old-fashioned *RAZR* phone with one contact stored in its memory. She pressed the number five. After exactly two rings, Ruthless answered.

"C-Mac want me to go to his crib with him. Do you want me to end his line today?"

Following a moment of silence, Ruthless said, "Yeah, end that nigga power line."

She began strolling back towards the VIP, looking like she didn't have a care in the world. And she didn't. He was just another body to her. She pulled the battery out of the phone and deposited it in the first trash can she saw. She snapped the body of the phone in half and tossed the broken phone pieces in two different trash cans.

She stopped to buy a drink from the bar, but this was not to drink. It was to knock C-Mac's ass out. She tried to hand C-Mac the drink because it takes 30 minutes to kick in, and it was almost closing time. She wasn't trying to give up no ass. She just wanted to off his ass and be done with it.

"Hold up, ma, my phone ringing." C-Mac reached for his iPhone 17. Benny's face stared back.

"Man, fuck that hoe!" He pressed the reject button and placed his iPhone back on the table in front of him.

"Everything okay?" Bugatti asked, looking over her shoulder. She could see C-Mac's facial expression had changed.

"Yeah, everything good, ma," he said, rubbing on her soft-ass booty. She pushed his knees together and started to bounce that big caramel ass of hers on his lap.

"Let's go. I can get a room for us." He knew Benny was about to call up her people. He had to shake them. She wasn't about to mess his chance up with fucking on a bitch with a 51-inch ass.

"Bet." Bugatti smiled and winked her eyes at Corvette and Jucci before following behind C-Mac.

Back at the warehouse …

Benny was sitting in her father's favorite chair in his office. She had been trying to call C-Mac or one of her men who were assigned to him. "Fuck! No one is picking up. Where the fuck are they?"

"Where you going?" Peewee asked, grabbing her by the arm.

"Get yo' muthafuckin' hands off me!" Benny spat as she snatched her arm away. "I'm not 'bout to just sit here and watch Ruthless kill every man that is loyal to him."

Stacy shook his head from side to side. *'Damn that bitch got a fat ass,'* he thought as he stared at her ass jiggle.

Just before Benny approached the door, she turned and said, "If I don't come back, then at least I died not being a pussy like y'all." Her words hit them like a ton of bricks.

"It ain't the fact that I'm a pussy. You don't know what's out there. You might be walking right into yo' own death trap."

Before leaving out, Benny shot up her middle finger and left with her shooters right behind her.

"Come on, nigga!" Peewee told his brother, knocking his foot down from the oak wood desk.

"Man, what the fuck!" Stacy barked. "Where the fuck we're going?"

"Boss sent us here to make sho she doesn't get herself killed, now let's go."

"Nigga, fuck her!" Stacy barked. "She is walking right into her own death."

"Nigga, bring yo' scary ass on," Peewee headed out the door.

"Fuccckkk!" Stacy roared, not liking the fact that he was walking right into a trap. He was used to his enemies walking into his traps, not the other way around.

Outside…

Benny and her men jumped in the six blacked-out Tahoe and sped off. With Killa and Pewee and Stacy right behind them. Stacy cracked the window and blew out a cloud of smoke. His nerves were all over the place. They hit the freeway listening to BigXthaPlug.

Killing is what both brothers were trained to do. It was their job, and by all means they were going to get the job done, even if it meant getting killed in the process.

Lil' Fred passed Benny the blunt that was in rotation, which she took two puffs on and began to choke.

"Damn, boss, you can't fuck with the big dawgs or some?" he joked and everybody in the Tahoe laughed.

"Nigga, fuck you. I can hang! That shit booboo to what them Dominicans smoking."

Chapter 9

Mayhem

Outside the club, the parking lot was too turnt up. It was packed with a bunch of bad bitches busting out their clothes. Fat asses were everywhere. Loud music blasted from luxury cars.

C-Mac stepped out of the club with Bugatti right beside him. He dapped a few hustlers that were getting it out the mud like him, then walked towards a high-priced vehicle. He pulled off with two black Range Rovers close behind. As soon as he hit a busy street, he sped down weaving through cars, going a good twenty miles above the speed limit. No police officer would stop him. Not in a Bentley. Anyone who could afford a Bentley could easily afford a traffic violation to disappear. He looked down at his ringing iPhone and saw Benny's face again. He decided to answer this time. "What it do?"

"Where the fuck you at? I been calling you all night."

"Chill out, ma, I'm trying to do me and shit. I ain't yo nigga, so come correct," he spat as he peeked at the eye candy on the side of him. Bugatti had her legs crossed, rolling up a fat blunt while gazing out the window.

"Bitch ass nigga, who the fuck you talking to? I'll have you touch right now for that disrespect. Yo' broke ass wouldn't have no motion if it wasn't for me. And on the strength for my little brother, I'm gon' allow you to live, but don't never in yo' life talk to me sideways like that no more.

You ain't shit without my family, remember that shit. Now where the fuck you at?"

"Damn, chill, I'm just leaving the Dg's," his voice softened.

"Meet me at the Whataburger by XTC 2.0 fuck." She hung up the phone in his face before he could reply. He couldn't wait to make enough money to shit on her and her family.

"You good, daddy?" Bugatti asked. He looked like he had lost his best friend.

"I'm going to be after you put in some work," he said, swinging his dick out for her to suck.

Two cars behind…

Ruthless sat in a black-on-black BMW 7 Series with five percent tint on the windows. The car was as clean as the plates on the front and rear bumpers. "Stay the fuck back some. We too damn close as it is," Ruthless barked at Lexus. She was driving the car. He decided to take out C-Mac himself.

"Nigga, whatever."

"Just drive!" Mercedes said, sitting in the back. She flicked the switch on the AK-47 to full auto.

Lexus pulled off slowly. From the passenger's seat, Ruthless looked back at Mercedes. "Get ready, babygirl." She nodded for the mayhem she knew was about to be served.

C-Mac slowed the Bentley down for the red light up ahead. Bugatti raised her head for some air. She had been eating the dick since they first left the club ten minutes ago.

"You like that, daddy?" she asked, looking up at him. She looked out the rearview mirror and saw a motorbike roaring down the street. Ruthless decided at the last moment to kill C-Mac in public. But really, he wanted to witness his death, hoping it would bring out the rest of Benny's men.

Jucci blasted out of an obscured angle of the street with a little dress that was hiked over her huge ass. Corvette was on the motorcycle, coming up the street from behind C-Mac and Bugatti in a small black dress that was also hiked over her fat ass. Both women had their faces concealed by helmets that matched their bikes. Corvette pulled onto the side of the Lambo. Her tires screamed on the asphalt. The sound echoed through the grimy streets of Dallas. Jucci pulled up in front of the Lambo. She had on a pink and white shoestring-looking thong. She made her ass cheeks jump and clap before raising up an Uzi. Corvette did the same. They both aimed at C-Mac.

They unloaded at him at the same exact time.

TAT – TAT – TAT – TAT!

“Get down!” C-Mac screamed as a dozen bullets tore through his flesh. He screamed in agony as blood oozed from numerous bullet holes in his chest, with no doubt obliterating his lungs and his heart.

Both motorcycles sped away from the scene.

“Let’s go! Let’s go!” Ruthless yelled to Bugatti She hopped out the Bentley with C-Mac’s blood all over her face and clothes and got into the whip.

Chapter 10

Death Squad

Benny watched as Angel's men unloaded military grade weapons off a big rig. All she could visualize in her mind was painting the city red. Her murderous thoughts were interrupted by a cold voice that startled her.

"Who was the two females on the bikes that killed C-Mac?" Lil Fred asked.

Benny looked down at her wrist. She read the words that were tattooed into her skin. **DEATH SQUAD.** She used to be one of them. She was a hitman. She smiled to herself thinking of her two best friends. Jucci and Bugatti. They shared more than just memories together. They shared a bond that no one could separate; well, no one but Ruthless.

Benny's smile quickly disappeared as she thought back to the day she caught her two best friends in the bed naked with her man. The sight made her sick to her stomach. Ruthless sat there between both of them with a smile plastered across his face. All Benny could do was cry and run away. She knew why he had done such an evil thing: her father made her sleep with the enemy's son. The fucked-up part was that she was going to tell him she was three weeks pregnant with their son, but now Ruthless would have to live knowing he had murdered his only seed.

"Boss, we got another problem," Lil Fred said.

"What?" she barked.

"Stacy is dead. He got killed last night in the shootout with Ruthless and his people. His brother just informed us," Lil Fred looked into Benny's hurtful eyes.

"Peewee and Black Knowledge are on their way right now," he added.

Angel looked at Benny with a sympathetic look on his face. "Everything going to be okay, baby, I got ya." He wrapped his arms around her body.

"Yeah, for how long tho?" she asked, thinking about what Black Knowledge told her. "It's going to get worse before it gets better."

***

Ruthless walked naked into Bugatti's room with his eleven-inch dick swinging from side to side. He stopped dead in his tracks when he saw Benny's son in Bugatti's bed, smiling back at him with the same hazel eyes she was blessed with.

"Why the fuck is he up in here?" Ruthless barked. "Where the fuck Tete ass at?" Tete was the babysitter he met on an app called *Urbansitter*.

"I told her she could take the day off. She's in the back room with her boyfriend."

"You let this bitch bring a nigga in my house?" Ruthless spat, throwing some clothes over his naked body.

Tete was a sexy, butter-pecan complected female. She was short and thick but didn't have much ass. But everywhere she went, she broke necks. She had on a small T-shirt with some ass-hugging boyshorts that made her ass look delicious.

She was sitting in a leather seat in the movie room with her Apple iPad sitting across her lap when Ruthless barged in, carrying a Glock in his hand.

"Where yo' nigga at?" Ruthless asked, looking all around the movie theater that was built on the second floor of his mansion.

"What nigga?"

"Yo' boyfriend, bitch, where he at?"

"He didn't come. Why you tripping fo'?"

"Tripping! Bitch, this is my house. You are my babysitter. This is not *Six Flags*, hoe. Don't bring no nigga in my crib." Ruthless stormed out without hearing shit she had to say. But later that day, his dick was deep inside her pussy, trying to make a baby.

Satisfied, he flipped on his back. Tete grabbed his dick and stroked him up and down. "Damn, you got a big dick." She pumped all the cum out before it disappeared in her mouth. She was trying to shame every bitch that ever sucked his dick in life. She gagged on the dick for a good minute before she came back up for air. She sat there, staring into his eyes and at his eleven-inch dick. It had veins popping out on every side. She roamed his muscular body, taking in all his tattoos that covered his entire body, and stopped on the one that read DEATH SQUAD.

"What's Death Squad?"

The words took his mind somewhere far away from where he laid comfortably in the bed, with Tete breathing down on his dick.

***

5:30 p.m. Dallas, Texas

SKIRRRKKKK!

The black F-150 braked hard, and double screams of rubber on asphalt sent shivers down a bitch's spine. They stopped in the middle of the street. Three women jumped out, grasping AK-47s in both hands. They squeezed the trigger into the crowd.

BUDDA! BUDDA! BUDDA BUDDA!

People scattered, and Benny swung the AK from left to right, shooting everyone in sight. People screamed and ducked for cover, but there wasn't anywhere to hide. Benny and the other two masked women had killed a dozen people and still were firing at the ones who were still breathing.

Ruthless stood over one man and read the words that were across his bloody T-shirt: *Johnson Family Reunion*. The man looked into the eyes of a homicidal killer who had just returned home free after doing time on American soil.

The man was breathing hard. *Who could do something like this?* He tried to search in Ruthless' eyes for some type of remorse, but all he found was death and pain. He instantly recognized Ruthless' face. He gasped, choking on his own blood. In the back, he could hear his family's fatal screams followed by gunshots.

"I'm sorry, Ruthless, that your mother's death was on my hands, but I had nothing to do with her murder. Cash and Black—" *BOC! BOC! BOC!* Ruthless emptied the entire clip in the man who was rumored to have killed his parents.

Present day . . .

"I don't want to talk about it. As a matter of fact, you can take off and go home, fam!"

Tete strained her eyes through the cloudy smoke that was in the air. She searched hard in Ruthless' eyes but didn't get anything back but a calm demeanor.

"Okay, fine!" she spat as she jumped out the bed, quickly picking up her clothes. She left with her pay and a seed growing deep in her stomach. As soon as she left, Ruthless entered Bugatti's room. She wore a tight designer dress that barely covered anything.

"Where you about to head off to?" he asked as he followed the slow, seductive movements her huge ass did underneath her small dress. "You know we at war with the Dominicans and the Jamaicans."

"Naw, nigga, you into with them."

"Oh, it's like that, now?"

"I told you this was gon' happen. They not gon' rest until you die. Then you got the bitch's kid. The whole city is on fire because of you. You want it all. You even wanted the babysitter."

"Damn, hold up. Why are you handling me like that?"

Bugatti's shaky ass finally ceased when she stopped dead in her tracks. "Do you really wanna know?"

"Yeah!" Ruthless shot back.

"Okay, you got me and Jucci out there trying to kill our best friend. Don't forget the three of us started Death Squad with you. We made a lot of money killing for Benny's father, then out the blue you kill him and his entire family."

Ruthless laughed at Bugatti before he said, "Bitch, is you for real right now? Why didn't you feel like this the day y'all played tug of war with a nigga's dick in y'all mouth just before Benny walked in?"

"You still don't get it; you are still in love with her. Why you out their killing everybody that's close to her? You need to be trying to kill the nigga that took her away from you," Bugatti shot back before leaving out the door.

Chapter 11

My Ex-Lover

Beyond the doorway was a huge indoor pool. Lil' Fred looked into the crystal-clear blue water and saw a pale form. He watched her for a brief minute. She wasn't her encyclopedic self this morning. She was suffering from the death of her family and the abduction of her son, but she was still trying to enjoy life until she caught up with Ruthless. The air outside was clear and dry, and the sun was brutal. She was the only soul in the humongous pool. Lil' Fred decided to get her attention before she thought he was on some weird shit.

Benny was swimming when she heard someone whistle. She looked back and saw Lil' Fred waving a gun. She quickly panicked when she saw the look on his face. She started kicking and splashing back towards the edge of the pool, and a second later, she pulled herself up. Lil' Fred's mouth dropped. Water dripped down Benny's naked body. She stood there with enough ass for days. She was tatted to the max; her entire body was covered. Even her ass was tatted.

"Boy, close yo' mouth. You act like you never seen pussy before. But what is it?"

"Black Knowledge here, boss," he stuttered.

"Okay, where is Angel?"

"He left an hour ago, said he had to handle sum with his men."

"Dumb ass bitch! Don't he know we at war?"

A moment later, when Benny stepped outside with her men close by her side, she saw a long line of black Chevy Tahoes pulling up in front of Angel's mansion. Every member of the Black Guerilla Brotherhood was armed with submachine guns as they stepped out close behind Black Knowledge and approached her.

"Good to see you're still alive," he said with a smirk. "Where is Angel?" he asked.

"He's not here. He said he had something important to handle."

"Umm, I see. Well, it's not very wise to wander about when a trained killer is on the loose."

Lil' Fred chuckled. He was really tired of people acting like Ruthless was just untouchable, like he didn't bleed the same color as everyone in the room did.

"Say, my nigga, do you find something funny?" Peewee asked. "My brother died behind this shit."

"It's funny how y'all praise this nigga. He bleeds the same blood as we all do."

"Do you hear this young nigga? Do you not know who we up against?" Peewee asked.

"I don't care who he is. When I see him, I'm spinning on that nigga."

"So, you think it's that easy? That's what's wrong with y'all YNs today. Y'all listen to this young nigga calling himself NBA YoungBoy got y'all thinking y'all can do whatever in these streets." Black Knowledge looked into the YN's eyes. "But let me tell you this. Ruthless will rip you apart with a flick of his wrist."

Lil' Fred laughed, upsetting the whole Black Guerilla Brotherhood, as if their leader was a comedian or some shit.

"This little muthafucka don't respect shit. My little brother is dead, and you think this shit a game!" Peewee barked, about to knock the YN the fuck out, but Black Knowledge intervened.

"I guess your boss Benny ain't never tell you the story about her ex-lover."

Benny closed her eyes as her men looked at her to discover a secret she kept from them.

"What is this nigga talking about, boss?" Lil' Fred asked.

"Let me give you a short background on Ruthless. You see, Ruthless was a member of the Jamaica Defence Force. And he later came back to his homeland in the United States where he trained with a highly trained man named Shadow. He was rumored to have over a hundred murders in Jamaica. He was rumored to be the FBI's most wanted criminal and still is on this day. So do not underestimate a man that call himself Ruthless. He is extremely dangerous," Black Knowledge said.

Lil' Fred was confused. "Why did he go to Jamaica?"

"Because that's where his beloved mother was from, bless her soul."

"It still doesn't make sense to me why kill Benny's entire family if she was his ex-lover," Lil' Fred pondered.

"The truth would be revealed shortly—"

"Enough!" Benny shouted. "What you going to do about Stacy's death?"

"That's why I'm here. Come with me to my warehouse."

Back at Ruthless' mansion…

Ruthless stared at a photo of a man with two huge men next to him, who had their faces protected by a clown-like ski mask, armed with submachine guns. He knew from the picture the two mountains of men were Peewee and Stacy. Between them stood the most dangerous man Ruthless had ever met. He was the leader of the largest gang in America with 35,000 men under him. Black Knowledge and the Black Guerrilla Brotherhood were a deadly force to reckon with. Black Knowledge was listed in Forbes 400 successful billionaires in the United States, but behind the suit, he was a ruthless killer who had his palms in every illegal operation there was: from arms trafficking, bribery, burglary, drug trafficking, embezzlement, extortion, fraud, kidnapping, money laundering, and murder.

"She's on the move!" Mercedes peeked her head in the door. "Are you sure you want to attack her while she's with Black Knowledge? He's deep as fuck right now with about a dozen SUVs behind his limo. The whole shit look like a funeral," Mercedes informed him.

"I'm not going to attack her. I just want her to relay a message to her lover boy," he spat.

"Well, they on the move. If we going to do sum, it need to be now!"

"Bet, get strapped."

Mercedes was about to leave when Ruthless said, "Say, where Bugatti and Jucci?"

"They're out trying to get at the next target."

"What next target?"

"That pimp nigga paying us to take out a target, remember? I mean we do got other contract hits that's piling up. You act like you are so obsessed with ruining Benny's life that you forgot what pays the bills."

"Don't fucking preach to me. I'm about to handle this bitch once and for all."

"But why?"

"Because the bitch knew her father had something to do with my mother's murder. She died right in front of my eyes by two masked men. The other man was Black Knowledge."

"And how do you know that?"

"The man I killed years ago told me. Over the years, it made sense. My father and Black Knowledge and Cash Indigo started Black Guerrilla Brotherhood, but after the death of my parents, Cash ventured off and started his own organization, Voodoo Mafia."

"That's some deep shit."

"After we handle all our enemies that want us dead, Death Squad will run this city," Ruthless vowed as he picked up his shotgun and machete.

The warehouse…

Benny followed Black Knowledge to a secluded part of the city to an abandoned warehouse. When they walked through the warehouse, she saw at least forty of his men all ready to die for him. They were all dressed in all black with army fatigue pants on. She looked around and saw a group of tough looking men standing in front of a black SUVs with military issue weapons on the hood of the vehicles. They were armed with assault rifles and Drakes. She had to admit Black Knowledge had his shit together.

"As you can see, me and my men are fucked up about one of ours getting killed in the line of duty. We not going to sleep until Ruthless is dead."

Chapter 12

The Room of Owls

An hour later, Benny pulled back up to Angel's mansion, smiling, knowing with the help of Black Knowledge and the B.G.B.H. that she would soon kill Ruthless. Black Knowledge had promised her he would call her as soon as he got word that Ruthless was captured or dead. He said it would be within twenty-four hours, and when he said something, he meant it.

Benny's smile quickly vanished as soon as she and her men stepped out the black Range Rover. All she saw was death. All her men dropped, leaving her standing, covered in blood. Benny placed a hand over her mouth in shock. She was glad all her other men stayed back with Black Knowledge and his kill team.

The sniper had hit his intended targets. For the second time, she was caught slipping. She looked down at three of her men. They each had a bullet in the center of their head. This was the work of a professional.

She jumped when she heard footsteps coming towards her. When she looked down the driveway, Ruthless came into view, wearing all black, toting a sniper rifle. She stood there in shock, not knowing what to do. She quickly tried to reach for her 9mm Glock, until Ruthless said, "If I was you, I wouldn't reach for that." And at that moment, three red dots aimed at her body.

"Where is my son, Ruthless?" she whispered.

"Don't worry about our son. You need to warn your lover boy that he's next on my list!" he said as he cuffed both her juicy ass cheeks in his hand. "I'm going to bring down everything your father ever built, bitch. Fuck you and Voodoo Mafia. But until then, I'm going to kill yo' pretty boy lover just like I killed your father."

"You'll be dead by then," Benny shot back.

Ruthless laughed in her face. "By whom? Black Knowledge's fat ass? Every dawg has his day. Even ones that think they can't be touched." Ruthless released his grip on her ass it jiggled as he backed away.

Once Ruthless was gone, the red dots stayed on her for a couple of more seconds, then disappeared. Benny ran inside and tried to call Angel to warn him.

"Wassup?" Angel answered on the fourth ring.

"Where are you, Papi?"

"Over at my mama's house, getting ready for her 60th birthday party later tonight. Why? Is everything okay?"

Once she explained to him what happened to her and her men by the hands of Ruthless, Angel promised her he would be fine, and that he was sending some of his own men to keep an eye on things until he returned.

Later that night
XTC 2.0 9:30 p.m.

All eyes followed Bugatti as she walked through the doors of the club, rocking an extra small miniskirt that left nothing for the imagination. She saw the manager, who was a short, stocky, black man with a bald head. He was standing by the bar, eyeballing her hungrily. By the time she made it across the club, her small skirt was tangled and twisted from broke niggas getting a free feel. She would have cussed them the fuck out, but she had a target to lay six feet deep.

"Wassup? I know you got my text earlier about me working here tonight," she said, brushing her long, silk hair out of her face.

"I did, but what you gon' do for me?" he asked, finishing his drink.

"I think we can arrange sum," she replied, playfully grabbing a handful of dick.

A moment later, Bugatti's pussy stuck out like a peach. It was fat and wet. She looked back over her shoulder and watched as the stocky, short manager beat her shit up. She was bent over the desk in his small office. The way he was fucking her hard from the back, you would have thought somebody was pounding on the front door.

BAM! BAM! BAM! Bugatti's eyes rolled to the back of her head. She was breathing hard, and her pussy was sore, but she continued to stay in the fight. The stocky, short manager felt like Mayweather versus McGregor. He continued to beat her lights out.

"Oh my God! Shit!"

***

Meanwhile, Ruthless had the sniper rifle sitting on a shooting bench, trained on Angel Rantiello's forehead. Angel was at one of his many Mexican restaurants, eating and laughing among his family. He was celebrating his mother's birthday. Ruthless was 3.2 miles away, looking out a CheyTac M200 scope in a high rise where he had a clear shot on the last blood male of the Dominican Diamond Cartel. Ruthless waited and waited, and then Angel showed his pearly whites. *BOOM!* He squeezed the trigger, forcing the rifle to hop off the bench. The huge caliber bullet ripped through the drug lord's forehead and came out the back.

"A perfect shot!" a voice said behind Ruthless as he gently placed a hand on Ruthless' shoulder. Ruthless flinched, not knowing how the man had crept up behind him. "So, this is what I trained you to do when you came back to the States from Jamaica? To kill the people close to you.

What happened to the first thing I taught you, which was loyalty?"

Ruthless didn't have to look over his shoulder to know who the man was; his voice alone put fear in a man's heart.

"First, you kill Angel Rantiello Sr, then Cash Indigo, and now Angel Rantiello Jr. Who's next on your list, me? You killed the family of the woman you loved. The woman that spat out your seed. For what? Tell me now, or I will kill you with my bare hands."

Ruthless had never disappointed his mentor. When his mother had got killed, the man before him took him under his wing and protected him and molded him into the ruthless killer he is today. He vowed to Ruthless' father, who was his best friend, that he would take care of his only son like he was his own if anything happened to him or his wife. And in that same year, both parents were killed. Ruthless' mother died right before his own eyes when he was six years old. Two masked men poured a bottle of grain alcohol all over her naked body and torched her right in front of his young eyes, turning her into a pile of heat and smokey flesh.

"Do you know how it feels to have to watch your mother, the lady who birthed you, and raised you, get brutally raped, and then set on fire all for a secret my father told her? And she refused to give it to the two cowards underneath the masks that I know were Cash Indigo. I got close to him and became his number one shooter. I made love to his daughter—mind, body, and soul. Even had a kid with her. Just so I could get close to him. So, I can look into his face and see the pain he caused me the night I was hogtied and had to watch the horrific scene before me."

"Cash Indigo?" the man said. "So, you are telling me Cash Indigo killed yo' mother. Who was the other man that night underneath the mask?"

Ruthless didn't want to expose the truth. He wanted to sit on it until the right time and the right opportunity. "I don't know. I'm guessing Brad Johnson."

Black Knowledge looked into his protégé's face to search the truth in his words. He wanted to see if he knew that it was him that killed his father and mother with Cash Indigo. He saw nothing but a calm demeanor. He decided right then and there to tell Ruthless the truth about his father and their secret society, *The Room Of Owls*. "Me, your father, and Cash were all deep in the dope game. I mean deep, so deep that we got the attention of Angel Rantiello Sr and we all formed a secret society called 'The room of owls,' short for the room full of wisdom. And since your father was the supplier for many states, Angel wanted to go nationwide, only supplying your father though. And Cash didn't like that one bit."

"Then what!" Ruthless asked.

"Your father discovered some rare diamonds worth millions down in Jamaica and wouldn't tell anybody but Angel. Then a few days later, your father and mother were dead. Cash started his own shit; so did I. The birth of the Brotherhood."

"Why did you keep this from me?"

"Because I just put the pieces together myself. That's why he had you kill Angel, because he knew Angel would expose him if he didn't split the diamond money."

"I can't believe this shit. I had a baby with a roughish bitch that knew her father killed my parents!"

"I don't know if Benny actually knew about all of this. Where did you meet her again?"

"Years ago in Jamaica. Just like her father had enticed her to Angel Jr, he did me the same way so I could be his puppet on a string."

It all made sense to Black Knowledge now. Lure Ruthless in, train him to become a weapon, and have him take out drug lords that stood in his way without getting his hands dirty. "Damn, he really did manipulate you. And I'm sorry that I wasn't there for you from the beginning."

"I don't need your sympathy. I'm not going to sleep until Voodoo Mafia and the Dominican Diamond Cartel are just a memory."

"I have Benny's men back at my warehouse right now as we speak. You killed one of my most trusted men."

"Take me to them!" Ruthless spat, clutching his rifle tighter in his grip. "I'll pay for the funeral," he added, and followed Black Knowledge out the building.

Back at XTC 2.0…

"Damn, bitch," Don One was behind his iPhone 17 with the flash glowing in the back. He was recording Bugatti as she cuffed a Cîroc bottle between her enormous ass. She jumped up and down, never dropping the bottle. Now that was talent.

Don One was a rival pimp of the person paying fifty racks to Death Squad to take him out. Rumor was, Don One had put shade on Pimpin' Ed's name, saying he was paying his hoes. Bugatti was on stage, literally shaking what her mama gave her. She had Don One's nose wide open. "I'm telling you, with a bitch like you on my team, I can make a killing. We can shut shit down. I'm telling you to fuck with me. Let a nigga endorse you, bitch!"

Bugatti giggled as she fed on to Don One's every word.

Chapter 13

Lost and found

Tears fell down Benny's face as the news showed pictures of Angel Rantiello, the last-born blood of the Dominican Diamond Cartel. She actually got the news a few hours ago by one of his lieutenants.

"What the fuck is you talking about, Brazy?"

"He killed him, that son of a bitch killed him!"

"Who killed who? Calm down and tell me who?"

"Ruthless killed Angel," Brazy yelled. "He killed him!"

Benny felt her heart tighten as if she was having a heart attack. Her whole world stopped at that moment. She had just talked to Angel an hour or so ago.

"How did this happen?"

"I don't know. It happened so fast. We were all having a good time celebrating Mama Rosie's birthday when suddenly, we were all covered in blood," Brazy spat, shaking his head from side to side.

Three days later…

The murder of Angel Rantiello Jr wasn't the end of Ruthless' madness. To make matters worse, all of Benny's men been kidnapped. She still didn't know how the hell her men came up missing, leaving Black Knowledge's warehouse three days ago. It didn't make sense to her.

She cut the TV off when Brazy and about seven Dominicans walked into the master bedroom.

"Mama Rosie put a bounty on Ruthless' head, but . . ." Brazy said as he shook his head.

"But what?" Benny asked, slowly making her way over to the doorway. She closed the door once Brazy and his crew all took their positions.

"Nobody wants to fuck with it. They think he's going to find out and kill everyone involved."

"What about M11?"

"He turned us down first."

"Fucking pussy. We gon' have to handle it ourselves!"

"What happened to your men?" Brazy asked.

"I don't fucking know. All I know is Black Knowledge said he saw when they left, and later he got a call from Peewee saying they got ambushed by Ruthless and his people. It all sounded like some fuck shit, if you ask me."

"So, you think Black Knowledge lying?"

"I don't know. I been calling Lil' Fred for the last three days now. I just don't get how Peewee managed to get away, but not none of my men!"

"Want us to get a hold of Peewee?" Brazy asked.

"Yeah, please tell him I need to talk to him asap."

"Well, a'ight. Mama Rosie still arranging Angel's funeral. She wants a private ceremony somewhere in the Dominican. She is going to lay him next to his father and her brother. If you need sum, give me a call. You got a lot of our soldiers patrolling the compound."

"Where you off to?" Benny asked.

"Got to get back home before my pregnant fiancée starts tripping. I'm gon' let you know when we kill Ruthless."

Benny just nodded, knowing this might be her last time ever seeing Brazy or any of the men with him alive.

An hour later, Brazy pulled up to his two-story town home that he shared with his pregnant wife-to-be. She was six months pregnant, carrying his baby boy. This was going to be both of their first child, and he couldn't wait.

When Brazy entered his luxurious town house, his eyes grew wide as fuck. There was blood everywhere. He quickly snatched his Glock from his waistband. He walked into the bathroom where the blood led him. He found his fiancée's head floating in the tub, detached from the rest of her body, which was lying sprawled on the floor, naked as the day she was born. Brazy ran and scooped her body in his arms. He couldn't believe his other half was gone. Not only was her head floating, but she had been stabbed multiple times in the stomach.

A noise came from behind him. He froze.

"Just kill me already. You done took everything else from me. Just kill me already!" Brazy cried as he held his headless fiancée in his arms, rocking her back and forth. His heart was thundering so hard he thought his ribs might have fractured.

Before Brazy knew it, Ruthless gave him what he wanted. He plunged the machete into the side of his neck, right above the collar bone.

Blood oozed around the stainless steel. When he tore the knife out, a thin squirt of blood followed it, spraying the bathroom, painting everything crimson. Brazy gasped. Ruthless stood over Brazy as he writhed on the floor. He was grabbing at his neck, trying to stop the flow of blood, but was to no avail.

Then he died.

Chapter 14

Wedding Planner

Before leaving Brazy's town house, Ruthless wrote **30** in blood on the front door. He stepped out to see a white van. Ruthless watched as the van stopped directly in front of him. A tough-looking Dominican man opened the side of the van with an AK-47 in his hand, but he didn't have a chance to shoot. Ruthless quickly upped the Glock out of nowhere, like some type of magic trick. He lifted it up and pointed it at the Dominican. He backpedaled as Angel's men's AK sprayed a hail of bullets. Ruthless managed to duck back inside the house. There was a commotion behind the Dominicans. A car pulled up with a bitch hanging out. She unleashed mayhem.

Lexus let the Draco in her hand go. *BUDDA! BUDDA! BUDDA! BUDDA! BUDDA! BUDDA!* The hollow tips ripped through the van and the Dominican with the AK.

"Drive! Drive!" one of the Dominicans roared, trying to hang onto his bloody friend, but couldn't hold tight enough as his body flew out the van. They froze up when they saw their main hitta get wet up.

Ruthless ran from the house, proving he was made of titanium. He tried to help shoot as Lexus rained a whole clip at the back of the van, but it was too late, and the van got away.

"Fuck!" Ruthless barked as he hopped into the car. "Call Bugatti and tell her to meet us at the warehouse. It's time to end this!"

"Bet!" Mercedes hurled over her shoulder as she ran the Dominican man's lifeless body over.

XTC 2.0

Martin was facing his small safe that sat behind a picture of him and Amber Rose. He was recounting the money he made a couple of nights ago. He still couldn't get his mind off the 51-inch booty that cuffed a Cîroc bottle between her enormous ass.

TAP! TAP!

"Hold up!" Martin shouted as Bugatti crept inside the office, standing there ass naked.

"What you mean hold on?" she said seductively.

When Martin turned his head, his eyes got wide as fuck. Not because she was naked—he owned a strip club—she was holding a Glock with a silencer on the muzzle. "How the fuck did you get in here?" he spat.

"Shut the fuck up!" Bugatti whispered as she walked up on him and kicked one leg on the oakwood desk, pussy inches from his mouth. "Eat this pussy!" she moaned, aiming the gun at his forehead.

Martin stared at her pussy lips for a minute, then up at the 9mm Glock with the silencer attached. After a second or two, he whipped out his tongue and licked her pussy until she lost her balance. After a while, Bugatti kicked her other leg up on the desk, now squatting in Martin's face. She bounced on his tongue and nose, dropping it like it was hot.

Meanwhile, Corvette's red bottoms clicked on the club's marble floor as she sashayed towards VIP where Don One was hooting and hollering. The way her ass bounced provocatively grabbed every eye in VIP, even Corvette's ex-lover.

"Wassup, Angel Eyes." For a minute, Corvette felt like the entire world had stopped. Only one person used to call her that, and when she turned her head and saw K5 sitting there, she put her hand to her mouth. "Oh my God, K5!" She hadn't seen her first love in a minute.

"What's good, Beautiful?"

After catching up on old times, Corvette sat there with K5 and his West Dallas niggas as they celebrated K5's welcome home bash. Six years was a long time. She looked around for Jucci, knowing once Bugatti killed the manager for extra paper and destroyed the camera footage for this week and last, it was about to rain bullets on their potential target.

K5 leaned over and whispered in her ear. "You still fucking with that crazy ass nigga Ruthless?"

"Some like that." She knew K5 and Ruthless had beef over some shit that happened while they were dating, but Ruthless or K5 never told her the issue. Ruthless caught K5 fucking her mama. The same mama that used to sell her body to men for drugs.

"Haven't you done enough to your daughter? You just had to fuck her man too?"

"That pussy ass nigga still pimping y'all?"

"Pimping us? That's what you think?"

"I'm just saying. That's how it looked on the outside."

"That nigga ain't pimping shit. He saved me from my abuse mama that used to let any nigga fuck me just to get high. If anything, he family. All the girls with him got a story behind how he rescued us."

"But we family, too. I was your first real thing," K5 shot back, looking into her eyes.

Out the corner of Corvette's eye, she saw Jucci moving in a hurry. She knew what time it was. The owner of the club was dead. Jucci headed towards his office.

"Bitch, is you ready?" Jucci asked as she stuck her head into the bloody office. "You been in here for a minute now."

"Yeah, come bag this money up and meet me at the whip. Me and Corvette will handle the rest with the target. Get everything," Bugatti spat, wiping off blood as she made her way out of the office. She walked hard, throwing ass everywhere. She carried a purple Birkin bag where she had the murder weapon tucked inside.

Corvette's eyes turned cold when she saw Bugatti heading towards them. She quickly grabbed K5 by the hand and snatched him out of his seat. She knew his hood nigga Don One was about to die by the gun.

"Say, where we going? I can't leave my fam," K5 said as Corvette led him out the side exit.

"I miss this dick!" she hissed, grabbing a handful of meat. "Where you parked?"

When Jucci hit the corner, her mouth dropped when she saw Corvette rushing out with a tall, dark nigga whose face she couldn't see. "I know this bitch didn't just leave Bugatti!" Jucci stuffed the stacks of money from Martin's safe inside her Fendi purse and pulled out her Glock she had taped inside of her locker.

Every eye turned when Bugatti's 51-inch ass came into view. Don One seemed to ignore all the other strippers surrounding him and his hood niggas when he saw Bugatti. He stood from his seat as she made her way towards him. Before any member of Don One's entourage could blink, Bugatti shot Don One in the face, and he fell to his knees, clutching at his throat. She walked up to him, pointed the gun, and pulled the trigger two more times in his body. The screams in V.I.P. could be heard throughout the club. Before any of Don One's men could do anything, Jucci let her Glock go.

FA! FA! FA! FA!

Every man in Don One's crew ducked for cover. They had two naked bitches shooting at them. After Bugatti took a picture of Don One's body lying dead to the world, she got the hell up out of there with Jucci.

K5 sat back in his big homie's all-white Benz. He looked up and saw a handful of strippers and niggas running out of the club, then he heard what sounded like gunshots. "What the fuck was that?" he shouted. "Say, I got to get back in there, my cousin is off in there!"

Corvette strained her neck, trying to eat the dick. She was devouring the fat muthafucka. She was doing her best shit until she felt the fingers in her ass decrease from its original speed.

"Say, I got to go see what's going on. My cousin and niggas in that bitch," he said again as he looked around the crowd.

Corvette pretended she didn't hear him as she continued to suck his dick. K5 finally pulled his fat dick out of her mouth.

"If you go in there, you gon' to die!"

"What you mean? People in there!"

"He's dead. We came here tonight to kill them."

"Who is we?"

"Death Squad!"

Chapter 15

Phone Sex

Ruthless' cell phone rang, bringing him out of his killing state of mind. He looked down at his iPhone and let out a breath of relief.

"Where y'all at?" Ruthless spat.

"On our way. I just got yo' text!" Bugatti said.

"What you mean? I sent that text an hour ago!"

"I know. We had to handle sum for us. Our hit list is piling up, and our six-figure clients are getting real fucked up with us for not handling what we do best."

"Bitch, I don't need you lecturing me. Get y'all asses to the warehouse and bring my dawg with ya!" Ruthless demanded.

"Corvette ran off on us, leaving me to die back at the club. Lucky for me, Jucci had my back!" Bugatti spat.

"What the fuck you mean she ran off?"

"Nigga, can you hear?" she shot back.

"Bitch! Just get to the warehouse!"

***

An hour later, Bugatti and Jucci walked into the warehouse where a line of tough-looking black men stood, holding AK-47s. Sitting in the middle of the room was Lil' Fred, naked and sweating.

He was tied to a chair. When Ruthless saw his two red nose pit bulls, Ugly and Big Ugly, being led in on a chain by Bugatti, he smiled a wicked smile.

Mercedes and Lexus stood quietly, knowing the death for Lil' Fred was about to be painful and slow. Lil' Fred looked at the two big ass pits that growled before him and blinked a fresh steam of tears from his eyes. This greatly amused Ruthless. Just a few days ago, Lil' Fred been all about killing Ruthless. Look at him now – bleeding, naked, afraid, and under his control. Being a YN and trying to act tough meant nothing when you had a gun aimed at your head.

"This is what's gon' happen to every Voodoo Mafia member!" Ruthless spat, looking around the warehouse. "Let them go!"

Bugatti did as instructed and let the chains drop to the ground. Before Lil' Fred knew it, Ruthless knocked his chair over. He tried to squirm away, trying to protect himself, but with his arms tied behind his back, it was useless. Ruthless' vicious pit bulls grabbed a hold of Lil' Fred's neck and shook it from side to side. They desperately tried to rip his body in half.

Ruthless looked around and saw Bugatti's sour expression on her face. She looked like she wanted to puke. He snapped his finger twice, and both pits came and sat on each side of him.

Somewhere in the city…

Corvette had her hair in Chinese bangs that came down long past her shoulders. She was a bad bitch, and she knew it. She looked over her shoulder at her bare ass and smiled. That bitch was poking out, round and fat.

"So, what you gon' do?" K5 asked with clenched teeth.

Corvette twisted up her face and said, "Nigga, I still haven't decided. Why do you want me to go against my people and help you rob Ruthless anyway?"

"Fuck that nigga. He mean you no good. I bet he's fucking you!"

Ruthless had fucked many men out of their relationship, but she wasn't gon' speak on another nigga's dick.

"I'm gon' ignore that," she said as she grabbed her panties off the floor.

"Where you going?" K5 asked as he watched her walk away. He couldn't help but follow the rhythm of her ass cheeks as it jiggled like she was twerking to an imaginary beat.

Back at the mansion…

Bugatti's thoughts were interrupted by her cell phone. She put her iPhone 17 to her ear after she looked at the screen, which read: "No Caller ID."

"Who this be?" Bugatti asked. The caller was silent for a while. "Hello? I know you're there." Bugatti waited for a response. She was about to go off when the caller finally spoke.

"What you got going, beautiful?" The man sounded like an Arab.

"Raj?"

Now she was the one who was silent. Raj was Death Squad's main client that spent big to take out his enemies. Why was he calling her and not Ruthless had Bugatti thinking. "What do you want, Raj?"

"Now, I know you're still not mad at me for what happened with us months ago. That shit is in the past. You know our relationship couldn't be anything but what it was: Sex. I'm a married man."

Bugatti closed her eyes for a second, and she was right back in the room with a billionaire that invested his family's money on massive drugs.

"Fuck, Raj," Bugatti cried out. "Damn! Don't stop! Don't stop!" Raj had no intentions of stopping. He continued to blow her back out.

"Oh shit! Oh shit!" Bugatti's pussy erupted. She squirted all over the place like a water hose blasting at full pressure. It didn't slow him down one bit. He went harder.

"Take this dick! Take this dick!" Raj roared as he slammed into her with hard, deep strokes.

Bugatti's legs started to shake like she was a full-time stripper. He held her by the hips as she started throwing it back fast and quick. Her ass went every which way. She could barely control her 51-inch frame.

"Is you still there?" Raj asked as he interrupted their memory back of the two of them.

"Yeah, but I don't know why you are calling my phone. Don't you got a wife you can call?"

"Bugatti, I don't got time for that shit. I need to talk to you about an issue I got!"

"What is it?"

After Raj explained to her what needed to be done, Bugatti jumped up and pulled a black 2X Gucci shirt over her naked body and walked towards Ruthless' master bedroom.

"We got a big problem!" Bugatti said as she watched Ruthless put a bullet in the chamber of his Glock.

"What is it?"

"Raj said he want us to kill Black Knowledge!"

Chapter 16

Bread Straight

Miami…

When Ruthless stepped into Raj's mansion, he saw him instantly. Raj was a well-respected Indian man with old oil money. He was dressed in green kurta-pajama, which was a long tunic and trouser. He was standing outside his balcony that overlooked the beautiful blue water. He was joined by a young, very attractive Indian woman that was covered in a golden silk headdress. Ruthless knew it was one of his five wives.

When Raj turned to face him, a smile appeared on his face. He took one last puff on the cigar before he went back inside his crib. He embraced his good friend with a kiss on both of his cheeks. Even though Ruthless hated it, that was the way Raj greeted. It was a sign of respect.

Ruthless looked at his long-term friend and saw that he had grown a full beard and hair. He slapped a friendly arm around his friend and led him down an enormous hall. "I see Bugatti gave you my message."

"Yes, she did, and I got on the first flight here. I want to know why you want to kill the man that taught me everything. Plus, Black Knowledge and your father have been doing business before we were born. Why do you want him dead?"

"Let's just say he's in everybody's way!"

"And *everybody* . . . you mean you and your father?"

"Exactly!"

"I thought your father was in the Middle East somewhere? Why does he care what happens here in the States?"

"My father plans on coming to the States in three months, but he doesn't want to go to war with a man like Black Knowledge so—" Ruthless cut him off.

"So, get someone close to him to do the dirty work?" Ruthless said.

"It's not like that, but my father wants it done before he comes to the States, and it's a million dollars when the hit is done!"

Hearing a million dollars, Ruthless had no choice but to show nothing but VVS.

"My man!" Raj said, "I got a surprise for you. Follow me."

When they stepped outside onto the balcony, Raj called over to the big booty Indian chick in their native tongue. She walked over, her face and body concealed completely. Raj said something in her ear, and a second later, she was taking off all her clothes. When she was completely naked, Ruthless couldn't keep his eyes off her flawless body. It was amazing.

"This is Riz, one of my wives. She is going to take good care of you. Isn't that, right?" Raj gave her a look like '*bitch you better do yo' damn job.*' She nodded in agreement as she took a step towards Ruthless. Her titties and ass bounced with every step. Ruthless had to admit, for an Indian bitch, she had a nice firm ass and some nice round titties that he couldn't see under all that shit she had covering it.

Riz grabbed his Gucci belt and pulled him into an enormous room that was elegant. It had marble columns and sculptures in glass enclosures, and the double-height ceiling was open to a beautiful, sky-blue sky filled with big, fluffy clouds. The room had expensive paintings everywhere. Raj had plenty of money, and Ruthless planned on spending it. The large, airy room alone smelled and looked like money, from the white marble tile floor to the elaborate lamps hanging from the ceiling. Ruthless didn't come from money, and he didn't have summer villas and private jets. But the muthafuckas he killed for had it all. It was only right they shared their wealth.

The bed was huge. It was where he proceeded to fuck Riz's brains out, pushing her knees up nearly to her ears to get as deep as he possibly could. He fucked her that way for ten minutes before she straddled him, sitting astride his midsection to press her large titties against his chest as she bent down to kiss him. He sucked at them hoes feverishly as though trying to extract milk.

He grabbed her round, juicy ass and opened it up so he could see his dick going in and out of her creamy pussy. She slapped his hands away and spat. "Let me ride you!" she stated and started bouncing on the dick like a Wilson basketball. She bounced and bounced on the dick until his eyes rolled in the back of his head.

After Ruthless was back dressed, he walked towards Riz, who had just put her dress back on. He grabbed her by the waist and whispered something nice in her ear. "That was sum good ass pussy right there, but I didn't come here to get my dick wet. I'm trying to get paid!" He walked right into a maid.

"The boss will like for you to follow me,"

When Ruthless entered Raj's office, the first thing he noticed was six drop-dead gorgeous women. They all looked like they came straight out of a Kite DM Magazine. He had to admit, Raj was having his life.

"Come sit, daddy," one of the women whispered in his ear. She had to be the baddest out of the six women. She wasn't even Indian. She was white with some enormous-ass titties.

Raj was sitting behind his large maple-oak wood desk, leaning back in his chair with his hands on top of his head.

"Did you have a good time with my wife?" he asked as he took slow puffs at the Cuban Cigar in his mouth.

"You can say that, but I didn't come here for that," Ruthless said, looking for any change in Raj's demeanor, but saw none.

"Good, Heaven, dear, go get that for me!" Raj told the beautiful white woman.

Ruthless had no idea what he was talking about. He didn't hear any phone ring or the sound of a doorbell, but a moment later, Ruthless watched as the big titty white bitch returned with a suitcase full of money. It was half of a millie.

"Thank you, Heaven," Raj said. Ruthless looked at all the dead niggas he fucked with before him and realized this was the biggest contract he ever had. Raj went inside his desk drawer and pulled out an FN 5.7 caliber semi-automatic pistol. "You see, this is an FN. A highly advanced firearm. I will like for you to have this," Raj said, caressing the gun as if it was a bitch's thigh or ass.

Ruthless looked at the gun in his hand like he was a kid in the toy store.

"We need this problem taking care of immediately," Raj said as he blew the smoke out of his mouth. Ruthless nodded and took the bag full of money and headed out of the office. When Ruthless got to the door, he looked back at his good friend one last time, carrying both the money and the gun in each hand, knowing the next time he saw Raj, he'd be a millionaire.

Raj wasted no time unbuckling his designer pants and pulling out his dick. He grabbed the closest wife next to him, which was another white girl with enormous tits. He put a hand on the back of her head and slid his dick in her mouth. All the other women crawled on all fours to please their husband. When Riz came back in, she slipped off her thong.

"Is our guest safely off the compound?"

"Yes, daddy," Riz said, joining the fun.

A smile appeared on Raj's face, knowing his father would be proud of him. He tilted his head back and enjoyed the many hands that reached for his dick. He had to admit: this was the good life.

Chapter 17

No More

Corvette

Corvette's phone rang with Ruthless' call. This was his fourth time calling.

"Ooohhh, daddy," she moaned as K5 finger-fucked her asshole with two fingers.

Ding!

"Hold up, nigga, this nigga blowing me up. He sent me another text message."

When Corvette opened it, she sucked her teeth as she read the message from Ruthless.

Ruthless: You need to get to the spot right now bitch, we got something heavy that's about to go down, and I need all my girls back for a family meeting. You are still part of this family, right?

"It's Ruthless, right?" K5 asked.

Her silence told him everything. Her mind was all over the place. She couldn't believe what K5 just revealed to her. "Bae, you sho you caught Ruthless having sex with my mama?"

"Yeah, that nigga took advantage of her and her weakness with drugs. He told me if I told you he would kill me, so I just left the shit alone. I didn't want you to be grieving over me killing his ass." He looked deep in her eyes and fed her bullshit. He was always jealous of Ruthless. The nigga had money and power. And five bitches that would kill for him at any giving moment.

"But fuck that nigga. We gone handle his ass. You gon' help me get that nigga money and I'm gon' off that nigga for you!" K5 spat. "Now toot dat ass up, bitch!" He gripped her by her small hips and finished what they started. He knew the Ecstasy hadn't quite worn off, and she craved the heat and pressure of his body against hers. She scrolled through her texts, and smiled to herself and lit a blunt, while K5 explored her body. The only thing on her mind was betraying Ruthless.

Ruthless

"Fuck! This bitch ain't answering the phone. I got sum for her! Once I kill Black Knowledge, I'm coming for you next, bitch," Ruthless vowed, staring at Corvette's picture in his iPhone. He was sitting in the car, reminiscing about their short journey together. She done picked her side. And he had a feeling about who she ran off with. He answered his phone once it started vibrating in his hands.

"Where you at? I got yo' urgent message. All the girls are back here at the mansion. Everybody but Corvette," Bugatti spat with a smirk.

"That bitch is dead to me. She picked her side. But I'm on my way. I'm leaving Raj's crib now," Ruthless push-started the engine to his 2025 Audi and burned off into the dark on his way back to Texas. He had a million dollars on his mental. He had Benny on his mental and all the other shit that was piling up against him. One being the death of Angel. His mess had quickly grown into something unusual – a top international man like Angel Rantiello. All the top boys and girls on Angel's mama's hit list were keen on killing him. They swarmed the streets of Dallas by now, waiting for him to make a mistake. For the first time in history, one man had the whole city against him, and they weren't the feds.

The only thing about surviving was how bad you wanted to live. Ruthless wrote down all the facts and the killers that could be used to try to kill him daily. He knew where they were always. He was gon' eliminate them before they could get to him. Starting first with Black Knowledge.

Chapter 18

Quickie

"Pee . . . Peewee, hold up," Benny gasped. His face was buried between her chest. He was devouring her nipples.

"What?"

"So, you are telling me Black Knowledge double-crossed my men, and he got them back at his warehouse right now?" she asked as she shifted her position in his lap to face him.

"Yeah, but Lil' Fred got ate up by Ruthless' red nose pits."

"Oh, yeah." Benny rose from Peewee's lap, her boy shorts were bunched deep off in her ass. His eyes nearly popped out of his head.

"What you doing, ma?"

"Hold up. Don't you want to get high before we fuck again?"

"Hell yeah." Peewee laid back on the bed. He had fucked her two times already before they stopped an hour or so ago for a break, that he didn't even want from the start. A second later, Benny returned carrying a semi-automatic shotgun. The same one that blew his brother's head off not too long ago.

"What the fuck you got going on? I told you the slime shit my boss done did to you and your men!" Peewee shouted as he hopped out the bed, dick quickly going limp.

"Whatever happened to loyalty? You only telling me this to save your own ass. I played you for this information. Gave yo' ugly ass some good ass coochie, and you got to singing like a bitch," she said with venom in her eyes.

Peewee didn't know what to say. All he could do was eyeball his gun that was lying on top of his clothes a good distance away. Even if he tried to get to it, he wouldn't have made it. It was sitting behind Benny, who now had the shotgun pointing at his chest.

"Look, Benny, you don't have to do this."

"I think I do. If you will slime your own, you will slime me!" She placed the barrel of the shotgun against his chin and pulled the trigger.

A thunderous boom tore through the hotel room. Peewee's face turned inside out; his entire head exploded. Blood splattered her face. It was warm, with a familiar smell and taste. Death was her second home. She lived for it, and Ruthless woke that monster back up. A cloud of blood and brains hung in the air.

She crossed the room and picked up his phone that sat on the table. She read over his message from Black Knowledge. The information presented to her seemed to indicate that Ruthless was on his way there to handle the rest of her men.

Chapter 19

Factory Reset

Benny switched past four tough-looking Dominican men, all armed to the teeth. She spun around and asked, "Where is Mama Rosie?"

One of the tough-looking Dominican men pointed straight down the foyer into the kitchen area. Some of her men began to applaud with each step she took. That ass was fat, and everybody with eyes could see. She felt a little disrespected. Her baby daddy was dead, and they disrespected her, but she knew they didn't know who she was. They were sicarios called in from the Dominican Republic to come and handle the man that killed Mama Rosie's only son. Other than her head throbbing, she needed a drink and something to eat, and one thing Mama Rosie loved to do was cook, and it seemed like she had been doing a lot of it since the death of her only child.

"There you go, I was wondering when you were going to stop by. Do you want anything to drink?" Of course she did. She just blew a man's head right off. When Mama Rosie handed her a glass of champagne from a long-stemmed glass, she bent down and kissed Mama Rosie on the cheek.

"Thank you."

"You are welcome. I'm almost done with my supreme double-decker tacos that I know you and my son loved." She stamped out her cigarette, her first in more than twenty years. Excusable under the circumstances of losing her only son.

Being nervous was natural, even for someone who prided themselves. At the moment, she felt invigorated. She felt dangerous. She wanted to kill the man that brought so much anguish in her heart.

"I got to head out to the airport to get one of my father's most loyal lieutenants. He's coming in from Jamaica. This is his first time in the States. He is a dangerous and heartless man. With your men looking for Ruthless and mine, we can't lose."

"Just promise me something, Benny."

"Yeah, what's that?"

"Please, bring my grandson home."

Benny stood there puzzled for a few minutes, looking into Mama Rosie's soulful eyes, and contemplated if she should come clean about Brazil not being Angel's son. But Mama Rosie interrupted and shouted. "Liam! Get in here for a minute!"

Who the hell is that? Benny thought, but that thought was soon erased when a nice-looking white man stepped into the kitchen. He was handsome and mysterious. Just Benny's type. But something was off with him. It was hard to pinpoint. He was tall and lean with carefully coiffed hair.

"This is Liam. He just arrived today from Great Britain. He is by far the best killer in the world." Liam had been with British intelligence for years before taking a desk job among killers. He's going to watch your back for me while he's here," Mama Rosie said. "And Benny, this is a good friend of mine, so treat him like you would me."

"I will keep you under my protection," he said in his baritone voice. Liam lifted his beige shirt, revealing a handgun stuffed in his pants.

Mama Rosie smiled. One would never have imagined a sweet old lady like Mama Rosie was a cold-hearted killer. She had killed more men than necessary without pulling the trigger herself. She doted on her kids and threw herself into her charity work, raising money for needy families. But within her closet were masses of people she had killed.

Benny and Liam did a slow walk around the house, getting to know each other. But she had to cut things short. She had to meet her Godfather. He insisted on coming, but she refused. Her Godfather was keen on meeting new people.

30 minutes later . . .

Just over thirty minutes after leaving Jamaica's airport, the jet touched down on the tarmac so smoothly it felt like he'd landed on a bed. Money is what he had been promised. Shadow got off the private jet from the jet, taking a deep breath of the city's air that was known for its violence. He bathed in the rays of a welcoming, lowering sun. This was his first time stepping foot on America's soil.

"We here, boys. We here to make this city our own," Shadow said in his deep Jamaican accent. He looked over his shoulder at his sons. They were each deadly and unique in their own way. "It is time to get at this cash and save our people." All six of his sons nodded in agreement. It wasn't nothing they wouldn't do for the man standing in front of them. "Nobody dies on my watch, but we kill as many muthafuckas that get in our way," he said, looking into each of their eyes. "The real Voodoo Mafia is in America!"

"Shadow! Oh my God! I am so happy to see you!" Benny ran in her Godfather's arms, wrapping her arms around his neck like a little kid. Shadow was a man not to be played with. He had killed more men in his life than the years she had been living. He was extremely dangerous. He started out as a hit man for Voodoo Mafia in Jamaica, but Cash Indigo saw something in him that was more than just a killer. Cash saw a boss nigga, so he put him in charge of the drug and sex trafficking he operated out in Kingston, Jamaica. Later, he became Cash Indigo's business partner. Cash ran Voodoo Mafia in the States while he ran them in Jamaica. But now the untimely death of his best friend gave him full control of Voodoo Mafia.

When he got the call from his goddaughter giving him the run-down about her father's death, he wanted to come right then, but she insisted she had everything under control, at least that's what she thought.

"Where is the rest of your men?" Benny asked.

"No need for them when I got six of my best shooters with me!"

"No disrespect, but we're going to need all the manpower we can get to go up against a man like Black Knowledge and Ruthless."

"Don't worry one bit. If they kill me, a lot of our best soldiers are going to cause chaos in the streets of Dallas," he said boastfully. "Where are all your men?" he asked, staring hard in the soul of the Spanish-looking men with her.

Benny introduced the four Dominican men. But Shadow's eyes drifted to Benny's enormous ass. Her jeans gripped her wide frame like vise-grips. She wasn't the little girl he remembered many years ago; she was now a grown ass woman.

"This is Mama Rosie's men. Her men been helping me try to find my son and get the revenge I so desperately want," she said, looking into her Godfather's heartless eyes. He had a dozen battle scars, tribal marks to the ones that died. He had at least six deep cuts on his face, and as she looked closer, he had a fresh one that she knew was meant for her father. You could barely see the many cuts that decorated his face, given the fact he was so black he looked purple.

"Do we have a car?" Shadow asked.

"A car? Cars are for strangers. You're family," Benny said with a wink. She was as sweet and down-to-earth as he could remember, but she was also deadly. He would keep his eye on her. They followed her through a door that led out to a large landing pad – and a large, sleek, black-and-white helicopter.

"Benny, really!" Shadow said.

Chapter 20

Cupcakes and Wine

Later that night
DGS 2:00a.m.

Shadow and his six sons stepped their way through the jam-packed strip club. He couldn't help but notice all the pretty faces and big asses. He scanned the packed club for any threats but saw none. A man of his caliber couldn't afford to make any mistakes. He watched as two thick-ass dancers twerked on the main stage. He had never been to an establishment like this one before. Benny just wanted them to relax before they go on a killing spree.

Shadow and his six sons posted at a table right next to the main stage, next to men and women with dollar bills in their hands. A huge smile spread across Shadow's face as he looked up at Benny. She wore a black hoodie that read "Slut" in big white letters across her chest with a low-fitted hat to match. Benny held her short black miniskirt down before she took her seat. She didn't want her enormous ass to be out and showing in front of her Godfather.

"It's a lot of bitches off in this bitch tonight. Make y'all self-comfortable. We have a very long day coming tomorrow. I need my men back and my son and the head of Ruthless sitting on the coffee table . . ." she stated as she mugged two strippers that passed. They were shocked to see so much money piled in front of the seven Jamaican men.

"Why have it if we can't spend it!" Kufu said as he thumbed through the bills he had in his hand before throwing them all into the air. Kufu was the oldest. He was thirty-one and by far the smartest. He was a 7th-degree black belt with a deep understanding of the art. He was super black and lean with cuts all over his body. He had a cut that went through his face like an X that he did to himself when he was twelve years old to prove to his father he was numb to pain.

Benny looked at Kufu and smiled. She knew if anyone could handle Ruthless, it was him, or his brother next to him whose name was Karate Sam. He was a 6th-degree black belt with over twenty years of training. He was dedicated to hurting people in the worst way. He was younger, more muscular – more exciting than Kufu.

When Benny turned to her right, she saw Shadow's youngest son Fox approaching with a big booty bitch named Yoshi Bear. The Gucci skirt could barely cover all her ass. She had just got there, and Fox snatched her up like a repo man would to a person late on their car payments.

Benny leaned in and whispered something in Shadow's ear, "I got to find my son."

"We will find him, chill," Shadow replied, staring at the dancer who was dancing for his youngest son. He had to admit the bitch was bad with some juicy thighs and a juicy ass. He loved the women in the states so far. And Yoshi Bear was a top ten. She looked just like IG model GoCeeCee with a phat, jiggly booty. Her measurements were 34-28-46, all natural. She had every Jamaican at the table injuring their necks in the process of getting a look at her. It seemed like she was under the spotlight. She jumped off the floor on her tippy toes, forcing her ass to clap together violently every time she bounced.

Benny looked over at Fox. He was the youngest out of six boys and nine girls. The darkness cast Fox's face in a shadow, but somehow, she could see him clearly. His powerful, scruffy jaw, his warm eyes, his messy dreads. He looked at her, and his throbbing, percussive eyes became her pulse. She was lost in them so much, she had to cast her eyes someplace else.

Just when Benny was about to excuse herself from Fox and his cold stare, she saw somebody that made her trigger finger itch. She tensed up when she saw Bambi pass her in the crowd. She was the same white bitch that was sucking on her father minutes before he was killed.

"Give me yo' gun, nigga."

"Give me what?" Shadow asked.

"Yo' gun! Give me yo' gun, damn!"

"Fa what? Who do you see?" Shadow barked, hopping to his feet and looking in every direction with two Glocks in his hands. When Shadow hopped up, so did his sons. All of them but Fox. He was too busy staring at ass and titties.

"Nigga, sit yo' ass down before you cause a scene in this bitch." Benny spat, yanking Shadow back in his seat. She was grateful Fox's dancer had her head bent down, working that massive ass of hers.

"I can handle this myself, just give me yo' gun and be ready to go when I get back."

"Hold the fuck up. I haven't even got my dick wet yet."

"You will, I promise. We're going to hit another club after this one. I got to handle my business right now though." Benny snatched one of the Glocks out of his hand.

"What is you 'bout to do? Should we be worried?"

"When you hear gun shots, duck for cover." She hurled over her shoulder as she disappeared into the crowd. Shadow's eyes almost popped out of his head once he saw Benny's ass cheeks hangin' out from underneath her small black skirt. Her ass bounced up and down like a book dropping on a hard surface.

Bambi walked to the restroom, not knowing her life was in extreme danger. She had her eyes locked on a message Ruthless just sent her. It said, "Get to the crib asap!" She smirked at that; she wasn't like his minions. She did what the fuck she wanted to do. And for that, her life was about to be cut short.

She walked inside the Ladies' room, throwing more ass than a major league pitcher. As soon as she tucked away in the fourth stall of the restroom, she heard the clickin' noise of heels making contact with the marble tile. What alarmed her was the clicking got closer. She was relieved when the clicking stopped at the stall next to hers. Her eyes drifted to some Giuseppe Redbottoms and a Fendi purse. She had to admit, the bitch had taste.

Bambi strolled through her Instagram with her many followers and gazed back down at the Giuseppes to make a mental note to fetch them hoes, but she no longer saw them or the designer purse. That was strange to her. She didn't hear her leave. Then it hit her like a sharp pain in the abdomen. When she looked up, her eyes stretched longer than Loop 12. She was looking into the barrel of a Glock 19 and the eyes of the bitch whose father she had setup.

"Noooo!" she screamed in a high-pitched voice like she was in a choir or some shit. Benny didn't hesitate to pull the trigger. No words were needed. Only death. *FA! FA!*

Her head tipped to the side as the other bullet lodged into her mental like a deep thought. Blood poured from her head like a waterfall, saturating her designer dress. The last thing she saw before death came to claim her soul was iridescent spots and nothing but darkness.

Shadow kept looking at the door, which his goddaughter vanished into. After the gunshots were heard, the entire club was in complete panic mode. Muthafuckas ran for the exit doors and screamed like the world was about to end. He was ready to draw his weapon. But the doors of the ladies' room opened, and Benny eased out with a smile on her face.

Chapter 21

The Meeting

"Psst," Lexus sucked her teeth. "Why do I always got to do the boring ass shit?"

"Because you know how to get the job done," Ruthless shot back as he paced back and forth in the enormous guest room.

"So, you want me to walk around in this?" she said, holding up the small maid's outfit. "I can't even fit this. Look at how small it is."

"Look, ma, this is our last assignment before we are filthy rich. A'ight, all you got to do is watch Black Knowledge's every move while I handle the rest."

"How do you kno' he doesn't know who I am?"

"Ruthless, I agree with Lexus; this shit is dangerous." Jucci spoke up, leaning against the wall with her arms folded over her chest.

"He doesn't know anybody in our organization but you and Bugatti and, of course, Benny. He never seen or met Lexus or Mercedes or Corvette."

"And how do you know this, Ruthless? You know Black Knowledge is extremely dangerous. He has connections that none of us have."

"How do I look?" Mercedes asked as she walked into the room wearing the same maid's fit that Lexus had in her hand complaining about.

Ruthless had to do a double take. The black and white apron was sitting on the hump of her fat ass.

"Now how the fuck do you expect me to wear that when my ass bigger than hers."

"Squeeze in it. This shit is going on with or without you!"

"Whatever, nigga." Lexus stormed to her room.

"Y'all just be ready and on point. We 'bout to make a million dollars." He looked at each woman that stood before him, knowing he could trust them with his life. As he looked around, he didn't see Bambi. "Where's Bambi?"

K5

K5 woke up and looked around the room for Corvette but didn't see her. He jumped up in panic and ran out of the room. He looked in all the rooms, kitchen, bathrooms, but didn't find her. He ran to the front door. He was about to run out butt-ass naked when the door swung open and in came Corvette.

"Damn, where you go?"

"What the fuck, why? I'm grown."

"Shid, a nigga missed you, bae." He lied, knowing she was his meal ticket to getting some real paper, and once he killed Ruthless, he was going to be up. Ruthless fucked the wrong people and now he had a bunch of money on his head. He was gon' be the one to deliver his body in a body bag. Corvette slipped up one day and spilled her life to K5. She told him how Ruthless took care of her and some more hoes that she considered were her family. He thought to himself that Ruthless had some pimp shit going on. She told him everything but fucking him on a daily and killing for him to earn a profit. After he lied and told her that Ruthless fucked her crackhead ass mama, she told him about the $250k on his head.

"What you miss so much?" she asked seductively as she sashayed over to him. She grabbed his dick and stroked it slowly while caressing his balls. He grabbed a handful of ass.

"What you think?" he whispered in her ear and licked inside her earlobe. Her clit jumped between her legs. She loved her some K5.

"Damn, Papi, you got me so wet." She hissed, especially when he slid his hand into her tights, cuffing both hefty ass cheeks with both massive hands. She led him to the sofa and pushed him down. She peeled her clothes off and straddled his lap.

"Ride this muthafuckin' dick!" He smacked her ass while she slid down his inches. And that she did. She rode him frantically, trying to make him cum. She would come almost all the way up, then slam back down. He leaned forward to grab a handful of her bouncing tits.

"Oh, shit!" Corvette shouted out. "Your dick is so big, it feels so good. Fuck me-e-e!" He didn't know how much longer he could hold on, but he knew he wanted to see her big ass jigglin' when he did bust.

Ruthless

When Ruthless walked into his room, his son Brazil was sittin' on the bed wit' his eyes glued to his iPad in his chubby hands. '*Where is his babysitter?*' he thought as he grabbed his iPhone 17 to call her, but instead he saw he had a couple of picture messages from her. The first picture he smirked at. It was one of her huge tits pushed together. The second picture was of her on all fours wit' her ass in the air and anal beads hanging out. A flashback of her talents swirled through his mental. As he held his iPhone, a new message was received from her. He opened it. It was a video of her pulling the beads out of her ass. It lasted only for eight seconds. He was about to put his phone away. He had business to attend to.

A new message instantly popped up from an unknown number. He opened it, and what he saw made him burn with rage. It was a picture of Bambi. Her face was caved in like something out of a horror movie.

Chapter 22

Matching Gold Thongs

Benny

Benny climbed out of the bed completely naked with a smile on her face. The sunlight that came through her window shone on her flawless body like an angel. She walked over to the counter and picked up her iPhone. She had a few missed calls and unread messages, none that were important. Until she saw one from Ruthless. She smiled triumphantly, knowing he got her surprise. She left Bambi with empty thoughts and a lot of blood.

Her smile quickly vanished when Ruthless sent her another message of her son sitting on one of his hoes' lap. The cold part was her son was smiling from ear to ear. He didn't even look like he missed her one bit. She took a deep breath, mostly because her son was alive and well. She had to get him back. She vowed when she did, she was gon' make it her business to spit in Bugatti's face. She was supposed to be her day one, but she was over there with not just the enemy, but her lil' one's father. She once called her a friend for life. Now she wanted to end her life. She was ready to make the city a morgue. And she was gon' do just that wit' her Godfather.

Shadow

Shadow got up from a wild ass night. A bitch got killed and he got his dick got wet. He looked at the strippers that made the impossible possible. He didn't think his night could get any wilder, but it did. After they left wit' sirens in the air, they fell off in *Pandora's* in Euless, TX. He was grateful they did. With blood still on Benny's hands, she took them from a crime scene to paradise. Pandora's had so many bad bitches in attendance he didn't know what to do. At the end, he took back two bad bitches, both wearing matching gold thongs. They were laid up on each other with big ass pillows all around. He hopped back in bed with a hard ass dick. Both ladies were driving him crazy. At the sight of their round asses, he kneeled on each side of them and ripped both of their panties away from their shaved little pussies roughly, like he did back in his youth back in his homeland. He was ready to stuff some dick in some *wet* when somebody banged on the door of his hotel suite. Only a few knew he was there. He was about to get on his sons' asses.

"Where are you going, daddy?" one of the strippers asked. She opened her legs wide, and the other stripper patted her on the pussy. "We need for you to beat this shit up. You are an animal." The other stripper slammed her finger in her pussy and got to fingering her pussy so fast she could barely breathe. She was real wet and juicy.

When he snatched open the door, he was livid. He was about to cuss whoever ass out. Until he saw Benny standing there with wet tears runnin' down her face.

"What is it, Babygirl?"

"Look!" Benny said, stepping into the enormous suite. The Omni was a 5-star hotel designed for the rich and famous. Not a want-to-be killer. "My baby is alive. We need to make our move on the warehouse to rescue my men."

"Let me get dressed and get my sons. I promise I will do all I can to get your son back."

As they walked down the hallway, she heard moans. He told her to let him get rid of his company. She didn't have to wait long. He grabbed the strippers' belongings and threw them out of the suite. They couldn't believe it. The thicker one that was getting her pussy fingered exhaled loudly and fixed her bra over her titties. As she pulled up her gold thong further up her round ass, she looked over at Benny wit' a mug on her face.

"Who is this bitch?" That was the wrong thing she could say at that moment. Benny calmly got up and walked calmly over to her and smacked her across the face with her gun. Blood oozed out of her nose and mouth. The other stripper got the picture and headed out quickly. Shadow walked over to her and looked down at her bleeding face. He didn't say a word. He grabbed the disrespectful ass bitch by the hair and dragged her ass out the room.

After cleaning up the blood, Shadow took a quick shower. He scrunched up his face and shook his head. All his sons were ready but Fox. "Where is Fox?"

"He's still in his suite with ol' girl from the club," Black Spider said over the speakerphone.

He was Shadow's fifth son next to the baby Fox. He was only twenty-one years old, but he was straight wildin'. He had killed four niggas in his life and was itching to kill number five, six, and seven. He was also a gifted fighter. But he was most gifted with any type of knife, sword, blade, etc.

Shadow closed his eyes and opened them back up. Fox was such a fuck up. He grabbed his gun and made his way out of the suite with Benny right behind him. She didn't have time to play any games. Fox could get it too.

Fox continued to pound away. He was holding Yoshi Bear by the waist and banging her for all he was worth. As he was about to explode, the stripper begged him not to nut inside of her, so he pulled out and busted all over her nicely round ass.

Boom! Boom!

Fox screwed up his face. They weren't expecting room service or any other muthafucka. Then he heard Benny's voice. It sounded like the devil himself. "Open dis muthafuckin' door." That got the stripper's attention immediately; her eyes widened with a rare expression of fear.

"Oh, my gawdd, you didn't tell me you had a bitch."

"I don't!" He slowly moved towards the door. The beating on the door got louder, and Benny's voice got madder. When he opened the door, Benny stood there wit' death written all over her face. She tried to peek inside the suite, but got an eyeful of dick. It had to be ten inches or more.

"What do you want?" he said under his tobacco breath.

"Play time is over."

"What do you mean?" Fox said, cockin' an eyebrow at Benny's gun in her hand. He just really noticed it.

"My son is alive. We need to make our move now."

Fox nodded. There weren't any words left to be said. It was time to kill, or it was time to die.

Chapter 23

Play Time is Over

Shadow

Shadow watched as a bunch of niggas walked up and down, patrolling the old-looking warehouse, totin' heavy military-grade weapons. "This is goin' to be a piece of cake for me and my sons," he said proudly as he gripped his high-powered assault rifle. "Son, take them out!" Shadow spat into his earbuds.

Kufu let the sniper rifle jump to life. He was probably thirty feet away on an abandoned five-story building.

"Let's move out," Shadow spat, hopping out of the black-tinted, big body SUV.

"Hold up, it's still movement out there," Benny pointed out.

"Trust me, not for long. Do you want to get yo' men back or not?"

"Yeah, but I'm not about to die," Benny shot back with a smirk.

"Trust me, you're not. I trust my sons with my life," Shadow said before takin' off with his sons close behind him.

Within minutes, Benny saw four of Black Knowledge's men's heads explode like a grape being stepped on. She watched as Shadow ran right past the dead bodies just before they dropped. Just as he said, his sons were professionals at a craft that was taught to them at a very young age.

Two niggas were clueless to what just occurred right in front of them. They watched from afar as four of their best killers dropped to the floor like a bad habit. Their mind got right once they saw niggas rushing towards them. They reached and tried to up their weapons, but unfortunately, they didn't even have time to scream as Fox brought down a knife, stabbing the blunt point directly into the side of the closest man's neck. When he pulled the knife free, a narrow jet of blood followed. Fox was laughing maniacally as he stabbed the other man over and over and over again in the stomach.

"Let's get in and get out," Shadow barked, crouching low by the front entrance of the warehouse. He held up his fingers to count down, starting with three. Once it got to one, they rushed in, guns drawn like they were the Feds hitting a notorious drug spot.

Once the door was kicked opened, there was a dozen muthafuckaz inside working, including naked bitches packing up work and stamping Black Knowledge's kilos of heroin wit' his "The Family" stamp.

Budddddddddaaaa! Budddddaaa!

A chaotic whirlwind ripped through the warehouse as everybody scrambled for the exits. Niggas and bitches were shovin' each other aside and clamberin' over one another to save their own ass.

Shadow aimed at everything that moved. Bullets ripped through necks, legs, arms, and faces. Benny was horror-struck. It was like watching an action-packed movie; muthafuckaz dropped like bad weather. There was one naked bitch with gloves still on and a white face mask pounding on the door, diggin' her fingers between the doors trying to wrench it open. "Come on! Come on!" she was saying before she got drilled to the muthafuckin' door. Benny's eyes immediately grew wide as they fell upon the carnage around her. There were bodies strewn all around the warehouse, blood having splattered almost every inch of the walls and product.

She watched as Shadow moved with the quickness. What he missed, his sons were right on it, putting a bullet in their skull. What really amazed her was how quick and deadly Fox was with a knife. "Ooooowww!" filled the air. Once all Black Knowledge's men were sprawled out, leaking blood and gore, Benny searched the warehouse for her men, and it didn't take long. They were locked in a smelly, hot room. She counted eleven, when it was supposed to be fourteen. She got them all uncuffed and yanked off the tape that covered their mouth. She knew from Peewee that Lil' Fred was dead. But she had to ask where the other ones were. He only mentioned Lil' Fred.

"Where are all the others?" She looked at each of them, and one by one they dropped their heads in defeat. "Is anyone going to speak up?"

"They're dead, Benny," a skinny, dreaded-up Jamaican said, looking down at the pavement. "They killed Lil' Fred first. Every day they would kill one of us for information about stash houses and your whereabouts. But no one said a word."

Benny was honored by her fallen men. They kept it G. But fucking with a man like Ruthless, more of her men would die.

"Benny, where you at?" Shadow spat, stepping into the cold, smelly room. All her men standing there looked in surprise. Each of them had heard of the notorious gangster before them. He did some gruesome things to his enemies in the drug trade back home. Even the Jamaican government feared him. They each dropped to their knees, praising the man that was the leader of the ruthless Voodoo Mafia Gang. They were heartless muthafuckaz.

"Where are the rest of your men?" he asked, not paying any attention to the full, bloody Jamaicans at his feet praising him.

"Dead!" Benny shot back as she passed him.

"Well, at least you got some still alive to fight this on-going war," he replied. "My boy Kufu is in the front, waiting on us."

When Benny got to the front of the warehouse, she watched as her Godfather's son packed up raw dope of Black Knowledge's product. "What's going on? I thought we were just coming for my men, but now I see your sons stealing Black Knowledge's drugs."

"Calm down, sweetheart, you worry too much." Shadow walked over to the big body SUV that Kufu stood next to, as his little brothers filled the large vehicle with enough drugs to give them each a life sentence.

Chapter 24

Dirty Clothes

Black Knowledge

Black Knowledge watched as Benny and her men stole from him on his flat-screen that was bolted to the wall in his enormous office.

"They're stealing from us, Boss, and you don't want to do shit about it. They killed our men, and they're stealing. Let me handle this, sir, please!" Foolboy begged as he watched Benny and her men walk back and forth from inside the warehouse.

"I said hold off; time is coming. I want to know how the bitch knew I double-crossed her and her men."

"We shouldn't have trusted Ruthless," he spat through clenched teeth.

"Is that how you really feel about me, nigga?" Ruthless entered the room, escorted by two foreign maids that looked good enough to eat.

"Here is your guest, Big Daddy," Lexus said politely.

"Thank y'all. Y'all can let y'all self out."

"Do you need anything else, Big Daddy?"

"Not now; come back later," Black Knowledge said softly.

"That don't make no sense," Ruthless said, looking at the two bad bitches as they walked off, jiggling more ass than keys. "When did you hire them, nigga?"

"A couple of days ago. Come have a seat; let's talk business."

Ruthless and Foolboy mugged each other hard before Ruthless took his seat. He had hate in his eyes and the devil in his heart.

"Can you excuse us, Freddrick?" Black Knowledge told Foolboy, calling him by his government name.

"What?" Foolboy couldn't believe his ears.

"You heard him, Freddrick," Ruthless smiled at him.

"It's Foolboy for a reason!" He glared at Ruthless with pure hatred.

"Enough out of you two. Now go on, Freddrick. Go get some of that new pussy I got working up in dis bitch." He smirked at Ruthless and added, "You can try them too after he get his nut off. It's enough to go around for everybody."

Ruthless already knew Black Knowledge's weakness was women. A man with his level in the game would be more aware, but he felt untouchable, and that will be his downfall. It wasn't shit for him to get Lexus and Mercedes to spy on him in a house filled with killers. They were his third eye. And soon he was gon' get his chance to kill Black Knowledge's fat, greasy ass. He wanted him dead way before Raj offered him a million dollars. He wasn't worried about the many killers he had guarding his crib; most of them were pussy. But he had gained enough trust to come and go as he pleased. Ruthless had only one problem, and it was Black Knowledge's new pet sniffing all around his ass every chance he got. Ever since Peewee went missing, Foolboy had been trying to take his position. Ruthless didn't respect him one bit. He wasn't no solid nigga, and he definitely wasn't no killer. He got that far up the ladder by being a yes man. As soon as Ruthless got the chance, he was gon' wipe his nose for good.

"What did you call me all the way over here for? I know it wasn't to show me no hoes. I got five of them at the crib."

"No, but for this." He cut the flat-screen back on that took up most of his wall. When Ruthless saw Shadow helping Benny, his jaw twitched and his trigger finger started to shake for a body. The last time Ruthless saw Benny's Godfather was when he was killing for him alongside his sons in Jamaica. That is what pushed him to join the Jamaican military. He wanted revenge, so for years he was under Shadow's care. He became friends with Shadow's oldest son, Kufu, and they both trained together brutally. They killed many men. They were loyal to each other, but Shadow was loyal to Benny's father for years.

"Where is Kufu?"

"Hold up; it's almost over," Black Knowledge said. "There he goes," Black Knowledge said as he came up on the fourth screen. He stepped out of the big body black SUV, staring right into the camera. He quickly threw up his fuck-you finger to whoever was watching. When Black Knowledge cut the flat-screen back off, he looked over at his godson, but all he got back was a calm demeanor. He never showed his true emotions; if he did, his Godfather would've seen fire coming from his pores.

"How did she know you fucked her over?" That was the million-dollar question.

"That's what I want to know, but I really want to know the exact time Shadow got in my city without a muthafucka alarming me."

"That nigga is the least of my worries. Tough niggas die all the time." Ruthless got up and headed towards the door to leave, but was instantly stopped by the hard tone of his Godfather's voice. "They just took out one of my most heavily guarded warehouses with at least $5 million dollars' worth of drugs in it within minutes. We got a lot to be worried about. Shadow is not to be taken lightly. He is a killer and has six boys that got his blood flowing in their veins." Ruthless never saw him like that before, ever. He was the type of man that stayed calm through every situation.

Shadow was a man that craved fear from men. Black Knowledge was a man with money and power. He didn't give man fear. They feared Ruthless.

"Well, you must have forgot I'm a killer too." Ruthless stared daggers into his soul. "I'll handle it like I always do."

Chapter 25

Blood and Guts

"Where the fuck am I?" Foolboy thought as he looked around the tiny, hot basement. He didn't know how he ended up there. The last thing he remembered was entertaining the two new bitches his boss hired the other day.

His last memory was sitting in bed ass naked, stroking his dick long and slow, while he stared at the roundness of Lexus' and Mercedes' asses. Both bitches were giving him a late-night special, popping ass and big ol' titties. He remembered throwing back a shot of Henny and watching as Mercedes crawled seductively toward him. After being dismissed like a servant dog in front of Ruthless, he needed some release to release some tension. He hated Ruthless so much that he could hardly focus on the scene before him right at that moment.

Mercedes took him deep into her mouth and began to suck the life out of him. She moved her head at a rapid pace, never stopping to take a breath. He leaned over and inserted an index finger in her ass and dug all around while Lexus gargled on his balls like she was in a contest to win something big.

Foolboy leaned his head back and closed his eyes for a second. When he reopened them, Lexus was moving behind him with her hand rubbing across his bare chest. He focused back down on Mercedes, whose head was still moving nonstop. She was eating the shit out of his dick.

"Damn, bitch, you can suck a muthafuckin' dick," was the last thing he said before something hard shot through his neck, and everything around him went black.

After Lexus stuck him in the neck with the needle, Mercedes stood to her feet and said, "Now, how the fuck do we get dis fuck boy out?" She threw her hand on her hips and rolled her neck, all animated. Her titties and ass bounced up and down. Lexus put one hand on her haunches with her head cocked to the side and mouth off.

"Bitch, I don't know. Call and ask your master. He is the one got us in these ridiculous ass clothes and doing this stupid ass shit."

"I got an idea," Mercedes said. "Help me put dis blanket over his nasty ass." Mercedes moved over toward the bed and turned and looked back at Lexus for a second. "Bitch, you gon' help or what?"

"And do what? Drag his ass out here only in a blanket? Bitch, be for real."

"What else we gon' do? Just sit here and wait to die? We killed Black Knowledge's second-in- command. There is a killer posted in every corner of the house. I don't have enough of ass and pussy to go around."

"Bitch, be for real. Look at all this ass we're totin'. You think they gon' be paying attention to what we're carrying under a blanket?" She looked at her dumbfounded. "We're maids doing our fucking jobs. As long as no arm or a leg pops out, we should be good. Let's wrap his ass up good."

Present Moment

Blood trickled down Foolboy's forehead. He couldn't wipe it due to his hands being duct-taped behind his back. He looked around and saw nothing but darkness. The only sound that could be heard was his heart beating through his chest like a pair of expensive headphones by Bose.

"Where the fuck am I?" he said in a weak voice. When the basement door opened, light came rushing in the dark room like a savior. He could see that he was naked and very vulnerable to whoever put him there.

He looked up to a man coming down the stairs with two vicious-looking gator pits at his side. When the man got into the light, Foolboy thought he was going to shit himself. Standing before him was Ruthless. He was accompanied by a thick, beautiful woman. She was dressed in skin-tight jeans that hugged every curve of her body. She had on a see-through shirt that showed off her erect nipples. But what caught Foolboy's eyes wasn't the goddess with Ruthless, but what she had in her hand. She carried Ruthless' signature weapon, a machete. She handed it to him.

"You don't deserve a funeral," Ruthless said as the thick beauty lit a blunt and held it to his lips.

After a hard pull, he looked at Foolboy and said, "After I cut yo' dirty ass up into pieces, my dawgs here gon' eat what remains."

Foolboy looked at both pits as they let out a low growl, showing off sharp teeth. They were ready to kill at any given moment. Just like they did Lil' Fred.

"After I kill you, I'm going after yo' boss. I just had to get you out the way first. You were really getting on my last fucking nerves," he said with a smile. He nodded at Bugatti, and she moved closer to Foolboy. She slowly moved her hands to the top of her jeans and opened them wide. She turned her back on him and slowly slid her jeans down. When her 51-inch ass bounced out, Foolboy's dick stiffened hard as a brick. Once she slid out of her jeans, she cuffed her enormous ass cheeks and made them hoes clap. She walked towards Foolboy, grabbing his hard dick, massaging it just like Ruthless had instructed. With one swift motion, Ruthless cut through his dick like butter. Blood burst out like a shaken-up soda. Foolboy kept squeezing his eyes open and close, trying to endure the pain like a G, but it was too much for him to bear. And after seeing his dick sitting in his lap, he lost it. Ruthless quickly took him out of his misery. He walked behind him and yanked his head back. He placed the machete on his thin piece of skin and went back and forth against the grain. He sawed through his neck deep and hard like he was cutting through a tree. Blood gushed all over the place.

Bugatti stood there and watched quietly as Ruthless chopped a human being's head right off his body. It sounded like tape being ripped repeatedly. He stood there with a smile on his evil face, holding up Foolboy's head high in the air.

"You are one heartless ass creature!" Bugatti mouthed off.

Chapter 26

Dirty Dishes

K5

K5 stared at Corvette while she got dressed. She pulled her black hoodie over her head and laced up her all-black Timbs.

"Are you ready, nigga? Once we run up on Phinehas, there is no going back." She grabbed her two Mac-11s.

"Hell, fuck yeah," he stated as two of his best friends walked through the door, armed and ready for whatever. Corvette scanned the room. She didn't know K5 was bringing in new faces to their lick. They agreed to no new faces.

"Who the fuck is they?" she asked with a lot of attitude. She didn't give two fucks about being naked from the waist down.

"Don't worry about it. We gon' handle our end."

"Whatever, let's move out." She pulled her skin-tight black leggings all up in her gap. Each nigga took notice and stared at her camel toe before getting back right. They had a nigga to get at and money to collect.

With three killers in the blacked-out Benz, Corvette could feel her trigger finger itching for blood. She couldn't believe she was about to fuck over the family that raised her after her T-jones' untimely battle with her drug addiction over some dick that walked out on her years ago, but she was in love with K5. But was what K5 told her about Ruthless even true? Did he catch Ruthless fucking on her T-jones? Was he the reason she OD'd? Her mind was all over the place. She needed the truth. She was gon' get it before she put a bullet between Ruthless' eyes.

"Who dat?" K5 asked, pointing at a white-on-white Ford GT.

"Follow dat car," Corvette demanded.

"Who is it?" K5 asked again, staring at the mansion where Ruthless laid his head, not believing a man got so much money off claiming a body.

"Nigga, who you think?"

A smile crept across K5's face as he pulled the Benz into the dark streets.

After a while, they followed Ruthless long enough. Corvette knew where he was heading. She had K5 circle back to Ruthless' crib. She was gon' take his son and demand a ransom from Benny after she dealt with Ruthless. She knew exactly how she was gon' collect her end of the bargain. She wanted a million dollars for Brazil.

"We been following this pussy for this long, and now you want us to turn back around. For what? What he got at his crib you not telling us about? You told me he doesn't keep money at the crib. The plan was to off this nigga and collect the honeybun that's on his head."

"Nigga, you need to shut the fuck up. The way Phinehas was going, he was heading straight to Black Knowledge's crib. I know he got more than one Glizzy. And his fucking car is bulletproof. So shut the fuck up and get us back to his crib. I got a plan to ensure us some more riches."

K5 ran a hand down his face and let out a long, frustrated sigh. He turned the Benz around just as he was told. They drove in silence, contemplating their next move.

Back at Ruthless' Crib

Tete, the babysitter, was standing next to Bugatti as she loaded her gold-plated Glock. She had just received a text message from Ruthless informing her to round up all the girls so they can meet him at Black Knowledge's shit. With Foolboy out of the way, killing Black Knowledge should be a piece of cake. Then they could collect the million dollars Raj had on the table and handle their real threat: Benny and Shadow. They were ending all their beef tonight.

"Don't open the door for nobody. Brazil is in my bed sleepin'," Bugatti told Tete as she tucked her pole in her waistband like she was a nigga with a dick or some.

"Okay. You just be careful."

"I will, trust and believe that. Just do as I told you. Don't worry; nobody is stupid enough to try us at our front door." She left out the door, never looking back. She had one thing on her mental, and it was blood.

As Corvette and K5 and them were pulling back up, a pink Land Rover was pulling out in a rush.

Their timing was perfect.

"Who was that?" K5 asked, staring at the pink Land Rover like it was Nicki Minaj butt ass naked or some. Bugatti passed them without a second glimpse. She was trying to get somewhere. Muthafuckaz drove by in Benzes all day in their community.

"That shit really doesn't matter. What you need to be worrying about is not killing nobody. We get the kid. His T-jones gon' pay whatever for him."

K5's two best friends sat in the back of the Benz quietly. Their hearts were beating, and their blood was pumping. They had other plans for K5 and his bitch. When K5 parked in front of Ruthless' crib and quickly surveyed the upscale area, his childhood friends were plotting on his downfall. They were plotting to end his life.

Each person in the car knew play time was over. It was time for business. K5 was about to show Corvette he was about that life too, until Corvette said, "I'm gon' call y'all when I'm in. I can deal with the babysitter."

"What!"

"You heard what I said, nigga. Stay in the car until I call you." With that, she got out of the car without too much more to say.

The car smelled like musk and cigarette smoke. K5 looked at Corvette as she walked towards the front door. Her ass wobbled back and forth. His best friends couldn't help but look too. One of them by the name of Trent said, "I think yo' bitch is playing us."

K5 scrunched up his face. "What the fuck you mean?"

"Nigga, she is handling you. We are sitting in the car while she goes get the money."

K5 inhaled the weed smoke in and held it in his lungs for a few seconds before blowing it back out. "Don't no bitch run me, fuck nigga." He opened the door and adjusted his Glock he had stuffed in his waistband. He was always so easy to manipulate. His best friends followed suit. They hopped out, ready for whatever.

Corvette rang the doorbell a couple of times before she heard a fragile voice say, "Joe, is that you?"

"Bitch, it's Corvette. Open the door. I'm trying to get the rest of my things."

"I don't know about that. Bugatti told me . . ."

"Fuck Bugatti! Open dis fucking door, bitch!"

"Okay! Okay!" Tete was scared shitless. Corvette heard a lock turn on the door, and then it opened to reveal Tete's lil' scrawny ass. She fixed her bra over her titties. It was apparent to Corvette that she was about to have some company. Out of nowhere, K5 moved her out of the way and slammed the handle of his Glock in Tete's forehead, hitting her ass hard enough to knock her to the floor.

"What the fuck, K5! I told you to wait on me in the car."

He looked her up and down as his two best friends stepped over Tete. He smacked Corvette across the face with the Glock. *Wham!* Then he choked her. "Bitch, you are not running shit! Bman, go look for the kid. Trent, look for anything of value." He looked at Corvette with a death look.

"This shit ain't a game, hoe!" he spat, sounding out of breath. Blood spilled down her nose, and she had a huge gash near her lip. He retrieved her weapons and said, "I played yo' bitch ass. Ruthless caught me fucking yo' mama and threatened to tell you. But I guess he didn't want to hurt you. Yo' crackhead ass mama died because of me. She smoked all my shit, and the next thing I know the bitch is dead. OD'd. That's what the bitch get if you ask me."

"Bruh, there is a safe over here," Trent said.

"A safe? Bitch, I thought you said he didn't keep money here?" He pushed her into the room before she could speak. She still was processing everything he just told her. In the other room, underneath a floorboard, was the face of a safe. A large one at that.

"How we gon' get that bitch out?" Bman asked. He forgot all about the lil' boy once he heard safe.

"Nigga, we gon' take the whole bitch," Trent shot back.

"What about the kid?" K5 asked.

"Bman, go get the kid. I'll handle this in here." He pointed his Glock toward K5 and Corvette and started letting them have it.

FA! FA! FA! FA! FA! FA!

Tete jumped at the sound of gunshots. She looked up and saw the front door was wide open. She was staggering, trying to climb to her feet. Once she did, she ran outside half naked in nothing but a bra and boyshorts. She never looked back. She had to get to a phone to call Ruthless.

To be continued…

The Ruthless Life 2

Coming soon

About The Author

Tommy Cook started writing Hood classics in 2015 on the Roach Unit in Childress, Tx. His writing has appeared in Kite Magazine #10, among other publications. He and his six kids and his wife, Roseana, lives in Dallas, Texas.

Lock Down Publications and Ca$h Presents Assisted Publishing Packages

Due to an increase in the price of services we have increased our prices. The prices below reflect the price increase as of 11/1/24.

BASIC PACKAGE **$699** Editing Cover Design Formatting	**UPGRADED PACKAGE** **$1000** Typing Editing Cover Design Formatting Upload eBooks to Amazon Upload Paperback to Amazon
ADVANCE PACKAGE **$1,400** Typing Editing (line editing/content) Cover Design Formatting Copyright Registration Proofreading Upload eBooks to Amazon Upload Paperback to Amazon	**LDP SUPREME PACKAGE** **$1,700** Typing Editing (line editing/content) Cover Design Formatting Copyright Registration Proofreading Set up Amazon Account Upload eBooks to Amazon Upload Paperback to Amazon Advertise on LDP's Amazon and Facebook Page

***

Other services available upon request.
Additional charges may apply

Lock Down Publications
P.O. Box 944
Stockbridge, GA 30281-9998
Phone: 470 303-9761
Email: lockdownpublications@gmail.com

Submission Guideline

Submit the first three chapters of your completed manuscript to ldpsubmissions@gmail.com. In the subject line add **Your Book's Title**. The manuscript must be in a Word Doc file and sent as an attachment. Document should be in Times New Roman, double spaced, and in size 12 font. Also, provide your synopsis and full contact information. If sending multiple submissions, they must each be in a separate email.

Have a story but no way to send it electronically? You can still submit to LDP/Ca$h Presents. Send in the first three chapters, written or typed, of your completed manuscript to:

LDP: Submissions Dept
P.O. Box 944
Stockbridge, GA 30281-9998

DO NOT send original manuscript. Must be a duplicate. Provide your synopsis and a cover letter containing your full contact information.

Thanks for considering LDP and Ca$h Presents.

NEW RELEASES

BLOODLINE OF A SAVAGE 1-3
THESE VICIOUS STREETS 1-3
RELENTLESS GOON 1-3
BY PRINCE A. TAUHID

THE BUTTERFLY MAFIA 1-3
BY FUMIYA PAYNE

A THUG'S STREET PRINCESS 1&2
BY MEESHA

CITY OF SMOKE 3
BY MOLOTTI

GET IT IN SLUGS 1 &2
BY B. STALL

STANDING ON HER BUSINESS 1&2
BY DG SANTANA

STEPPERS 1,2&3
THE REAL BADDIES OF CHI-RAQ
BY KING RIO

THE LANE 1&2
BY KEN-KEN SPENCE

THUG OF SPADES 1&2
LOVE IN THE TRENCHES 2
CORNER BOYS
BY COREY ROBINSON

TIL DEATH 3
BY ARYANNA

THE BIRTH OF A GANGSTER 4
BY DELMONT PLAYER

PRODUCT OF THE STREETS 1-3
BY DEMOND "MONEY" ANDERSON

NO TIME FOR ERROR
BY KEESE

MONEY HUNGRY DEMONS 1-2
BY TRANAY ADAMS

HUB CITY MENACE 1-3
BY J. WHITE

A THUGGISH PASSION 1&2
LAND OF DA HOOLIGANZ 1-4
KILLAZ ON STANDBY 1&2
BY IRA B.

FO'EVA ROLLIN 1&2
BY ASSA RAYMOND BAKER

THE LEVEL UP 1&3
BY LUXURY KING

Coming Soon from Lock Down Publications/Ca$h Presents

IF YOU CROSS ME ONCE 6
ANGEL V
By Anthony Fields

A THUGS STREET PRINCESS 3
By Meesha

CORNER BOYS 2
By Corey Robinson

THA TAKEOVER
By Keith Chandler

BETRAYAL OF A G 2
By Ray Vinci

SAVAGE FAMILY EMPIRE 1&2
SOULLESS GOON 1,2&3
THE DIRTY SIDE OF MONEY 1,2&3
By Prince

FOR MY ENEMY'S SAKE
AMBITIONS OF A SLIDER
FRESH OFF DA PORCH
By IRA B.

BY THE TRUCKLOAD 1-4
TIPPIN' THE SCALES 1-3
BAD BITCHES WIT GUNZ 3
PROBLEM SOLVED 2
By Christopher "Diesel" Hornezes

Available Now

RESTRAINING ORDER 1 & 2
By **CA$H & Coffee**

LOVE KNOWS NO BOUNDARIES 1-3
By **Coffee**

RAISED AS A GOON I, II, III & IV
BRED BY THE SLUMS I, II, III
BLAST FOR ME I & II
ROTTEN TO THE CORE I II III
A BRONX TALE I, II, III
DUFFLE BAG CARTEL I II III IV V VI
HEARTLESS GOON I II III IV V
A SAVAGE DOPEBOY I II
DRUG LORDS I II III
CUTTHROAT MAFIA I II
KING OF THE TRENCHES
By **Ghost**

LAY IT DOWN I & II
LAST OF A DYING BREED I II
BLOOD STAINS OF A SHOTTA I & II III
By **Jamaica**

LOYAL TO THE GAME I II III
LIFE OF SIN I, II III
By **TJ & Jelissa**

IF LOVING HIM IS WRONG…I & II
LOVE ME EVEN WHEN IT HURTS I II III
By **Jelissa**

PUSH IT TO THE LIMIT
By **Bre' Hayes**

BLOODY COMMAS I & II
SKI MASK CARTEL I, II & III
KING OF NEW YORK I II, III IV V
RISE TO POWER I II III
COKE KINGS I II III IV V
BORN HEARTLESS I II III IV
KING OF THE TRAP I II
By **T.J. Edwards**

WHEN THE STREETS CLAP BACK I & II III
THE HEART OF A SAVAGE I II III IV
MONEY MAFIA I II
LOYAL TO THE SOIL I II III
By **Jibril Williams**

A DISTINGUISHED THUG STOLE MY HEART I II & III
LOVE SHOULDN'T HURT I II III IV
RENEGADE BOYS 1-4
PAID IN KARMA 1-3
SAVAGE STORMS 1-3
AN UNFORESEEN LOVE 1-3
BABY, I'M WINTERTIME COLD 1-3
A THUG'S STREET PRINCESS 1&2
By **Meesha**

A GANGSTER'S CODE 1-3
A GANGSTER'S SYN 1-3
THE SAVAGE LIFE 1-3
CHAINED TO THE STREETS 1-3
BLOOD ON THE MONEY 1-3
A GANGSTA'S PAIN 1-3
BEAUTIFUL LIES AND UGLY TRUTHS
CHURCH IN THESE STREETS
By **J-Blunt**

CUM FOR ME 1-8
An LDP Erotica Collaboration

BLOOD OF A BOSS 1-5
SHADOWS OF THE GAME
TRAP BASTARD
By **Askari**

THE STREETS BLEED MURDER 1-3
THE HEART OF A GANGSTA 1-3
By **Jerry Jackson**

WHEN A GOOD GIRL GOES BAD
By **Adrienne**

THE COST OF LOYALTY 1-3
By **Kweli**

BRIDE OF A HUSTLA 1-3
THE FETTI GIRLS 1-3
CORRUPTED BY A GANGSTA 1-4
BLINDED BY HIS LOVE
THE PRICE YOU PAY FOR LOVE 1-3
DOPE GIRL MAGIC 1-3
By **Destiny Skai**

A KINGPIN'S AMBITION
A KINGPIN'S AMBITION II
I MURDER FOR THE DOUGH
By **Ambitious**

TRUE SAVAGE 1-7
DOPE BOY MAGIC 1-3
MIDNIGHT CARTEL 1-3
CITY OF KINGZ 1&2
NIGHTMARE ON SILENT AVE
THE PLUG OF LIL MEXICO 1&2
CLASSIC CITY
By **Chris Green**

A GANGSTER'S REVENGE 1-4
THE BOSS MAN'S DAUGHTERS 1-5
A SAVAGE LOVE 1&2
BAE BELONGS TO ME 1&2
A HUSTLER'S DECEIT 1-3
WHAT BAD BITCHES DO 1-3
SOUL OF A MONSTER 1-3
KILL ZONE
A DOPE BOY'S QUEEN 1-3
TIL DEATH 1-3
IMMA DIE BOUT MINE 1-6
DYING FOR LIKES
By **Aryanna**

A DOPEBOY'S PRAYER
By **Eddie "Wolf" Lee**

THE KING CARTEL 1-3
By **Frank Gresham**

THESE NIGGAS AIN'T LOYAL 1-3
By **Nikki Tee**

GANGSTA SHYT 1-3
By **CATO**

THE ULTIMATE BETRAYAL
By **Phoenix**

BOSS'N UP 1-3
By **Royal Nicole**

I LOVE YOU TO DEATH
By **Destiny J**

I RIDE FOR MY HITTA
I STILL RIDE FOR MY HITTA
By **Misty Holt**

LOVE & CHASIN' PAPER
By **Qay Crockett**

TO DIE IN VAIN
SINS OF A HUSTLA
By **ASAD**

BROOKLYN HUSTLAZ
By **Boogsy Morina**

BROOKLYN ON LOCK 1 & 2
By **Sonovia**

GANGSTA CITY
By **Teddy Duke**

A DRUG KING AND HIS DIAMOND 1-3
A DOPEMAN'S RICHES
HER MAN, MINE'S TOO 1&2
CASH MONEY HO'S
THE WIFEY I USED TO BE 1&2
PRETTY GIRLS DO NASTY THINGS
By **Nicole Goosby**

LIPSTICK KILLAH 1-3
CRIME OF PASSION 1-3
FRIEND OR FOE 1-3
By **Mimi**

TRAPHOUSE KING 1-3
KINGPIN KILLAZ 1-3
STREET KINGS 1&2
PAID IN BLOOD 1&2
CARTEL KILLAZ 1-3
DOPE GODS 1&2
By **Hood Rich**

THE STREETS ARE CALLING
By **Duquie Wilson**

STEADY MOBBN' 1-3
THE STREETS STAINED MY SOUL 1-3
By **Marcellus Allen**

WHO SHOT YA 1-3
SON OF A DOPE FIEND 1-4
HEAVEN GOT A GHETTO 1&2
SKI MASK MONEY 1&2
By **Renta**

GORILLAZ IN THE BAY 1-4
TEARS OF A GANGSTA 1/&2
3X KRAZY 1&2
STRAIGHT BEAST MODE 1&2
By **DE'KARI**

TRIGGADALE 1-3
MURDA WAS THE CASE 1-3
By **Elijah R. Freeman**

SLAUGHTER GANG 1-3
RUTHLESS HEART 1-3
By **Willie Slaughter**

GOD BLESS THE TRAPPERS 1-3
THESE SCANDALOUS STREETS 1-3
FEAR MY GANGSTA 1-5
THESE STREETS DON'T LOVE NOBODY 1-2
BURY ME A G 1-5
A GANGSTA'S EMPIRE 1-4
THE DOPEMAN'S BODYGAURD 1&2
THE REALEST KILLAZ 1-3
THE LAST OF THE OGS 1-3
By **Tranay Adams**

MARRIED TO A BOSS 1-3
By **Destiny Skai & Chris Green**

KINGZ OF THE GAME 1-7
CRIME BOSS 1-4
By **Playa Ray**

FUK SHYT
By **Blakk Diamond**

DON'T F#CK WITH MY HEART 1&2
By **Linnea**

ADDICTED TO THE DRAMA 1-3
IN THE ARM OF HIS BOSS
By **Jamila**

LOYALTY AIN'T PROMISED 1&2
By **Keith Williams**

YAYO 1-4
A SHOOTER'S AMBITION 1&2
BRED IN THE GAME
By **S. Allen**

TRAP GOD 1-3
RICH $AVAGE 1-3
MONEY IN THE GRAVE 1-3
CARTEL MONEY 1&2
By **Martell Troublesome Bolden**

FOREVER GANGSTA 1&2
GLOCKS ON SATIN SHEETS 1&2
By **Adrian Dulan**

TOE TAGZ 1-4
LEVELS TO THIS SHYT 1&2
IT'S JUST ME AND YOU
By **Ah'Million**

KINGPIN DREAMS 1-3
RAN OFF ON DA PLUG
By **Paper Boi Rari**

THE STREETS MADE ME 1-3
By **Larry D. Wright**

CONFESSIONS OF A GANGSTA 1-4
CONFESSIONS OF A JACKBOY 1-3
CONFESSIONS OF A HITMAN
CONFESSIONS OF A DOPE BOY
By **Nicholas Lock**

I'M NOTHING WITHOUT HIS LOVE
SINS OF A THUG
TO THE THUG I LOVED BEFORE
A GANGSTA SAVED XMAS
IN A HUSTLER I TRUST
By **Monet Dragun**

QUIET MONEY 1-3
THUG LIFE 1-3
EXTENDED CLIP 1&2
A GANGSTA'S PARADISE
By **Trai'Quan**

CAUGHT UP IN THE LIFE 1-3
THE STREETS NEVER LET GO 1-3
By **Robert Baptiste**

NEW TO THE GAME 1-3
MONEY, MURDER & MEMORIES 1-3
By **Malik D. Rice**

CREAM 2-3
THE STREETS WILL TALK
By **Yolanda Moore**

THE STREETS WILL NEVER CLOSE 1-3
By **K'ajji**

LIFE OF A SAVAGE 1-4
A GANGSTA'S QUR'AN 1-4
MURDA SEASON 1-3
GANGLAND CARTEL 1-3
CHI'RAQ GANGSTAS 1-4
KILLERS ON ELM STREET 1-3
JACK BOYZ N DA BRONX 1-3
A DOPEBOY'S DREAM 1-3
JACK BOYS VS DOPE BOYS 1-3
COKE GIRLZ
COKE BOYS
SOSA GANG 1&2
BRONX SAVAGES
BODYMORE KINGPINS
BLOOD OF A GOON
By **Romell Tukes**

CONCRETE KILLA 1-3
VICIOUS LOYALTY 1-3
BLOODY MONEY BAGS
By **Kingpen**

THE ULTIMATE SACRIFICE 1-6
KHADIFI
IF YOU CROSS ME ONCE 1-3
ANGEL 1-4
IN THE BLINK OF AN EYE
By **Anthony Fields**

THE LIFE OF A HOOD STAR
By **Ca$h & Rashia Wilson**

NIGHTMARES OF A HUSTLA 1-3
BLOOD AND GAMES 1&2
By **King Dream**

GHOST MOB
By **Stilloan Robinson**

HARD AND RUTHLESS 1&2
MOB TOWN 251
THE BILLIONAIRE BENTLEYS 1-3
REAL G'S MOVE IN SILENCE
By **Von Diesel**

MOB TIES 1-7
SOUL OF A HUSTLER, HEART OF A KILLER 1-3
GORILLAZ IN THE TRENCHES
OOPS CRY TOO 1&2
THE DAUGHTER OF A CARTEL BOSS
By **SayNoMore**

BODYMORE MURDERLAND 1-3
THE BIRTH OF A GANGSTER 1-4
By **Delmont Player**

FOR THE LOVE OF A BOSS 1&2
By **C. D. Blue**

KILLA KOUNTY 1-5
TENDER
By **Khufu**

MOBBED UP 1-4
THE BRICK MAN 1-5
THE COCAINE PRINCESS 1-10
STEPPERS 1-3
SUPER GREMLIN 1-4
A GANGSTA'S SON
By **King Rio**

MONEY GAME 1&2
By **Smoove Dolla**

A GANGSTA'S KARMA 1-5
By **FLAME**

KING OF THE TRENCHES 1-3
By **GHOST & TRANAY ADAMS**

BAD BITCHES WIT GUNZ 1&2
PROBLEM SOLVED
By "Christopher Diesel" Hornezes

QUEEN OF THE ZOO 1&2
By **Black Migo**

GRIMEY WAYS 1-3
BETRAYAL OF A G
By **Ray Vinci**

XMAS WITH AN ATL SHOOTER
By **Ca$h & Destiny Skai**

KING KILLA 1&2
By **Vincent "Vitto" Holloway**

BETRAYAL OF A THUG 1&2
By **Fre$h**

COUNTDOWN OF A KILLA 1&2
SEX, MURDER AND GOD 1&2
GUNS DOWN, BOTTOMS UP 1&2
By Lo-Life

THE MURDER QUEENS 1-7
By **Michael Gallon**

FOR THE LOVE OF BLOOD 1-4
By **Jamel Mitchell**

HOOD CONSIGLIERE 1&2
NO TIME FOR ERROR
By **Keese**

PROTÉGÉ OF A LEGEND 1,2&3
LOVE IN THE TRENCHES 1&2
By **Corey Robinson**

THE PLUG'S RUTHLESS DAUGHTER 1&2
By **Tony Daniels**

BORN IN THE GRAVE 1-3
CRIME PAYS
By **Self Made Tay**

MOAN IN MY MOUTH
By **XTASY**

TORN BETWEEN A GANGSTER AND A GENTLEMAN
By **J-BLUNT & Miss Kim**

LOYALTY IS EVERYTHING 1-3
CITY OF SMOKE 1-3
By **Molotti**

HERE TODAY GONE TOMORROW 1&2
By **Fly Rock**

WOMEN LIE MEN LIE 1-4
FIFTY SHADES OF SNOW 1-3
STACK BEFORE YOU SPLURGE
GIRLS FALL LIKE DOMINOES
NAÏVE TO THE STREETS
By **ROY MILLIGAN**

PILLOW PRINCESS
By **S. Hawkins**

THE BUTTERFLY MAFIA 1-3
SALUTE MY SAVAGERY 1&2
By **Fumiya Payne**

THE LANE 1&2
By Ken-Ken Spence

THE PUSSY TRAP 1-5
By **Nene Capri**

DIRTY DNA
By **Blaque**

SANCTIFIED AND HORNY
by **XTASY**

BOOKS BY LDP'S CEO, CA$H

TRUST IN NO MAN
TRUST IN NO MAN 2
TRUST IN NO MAN 3
BONDED BY BLOOD
SHORTY GOT A THUG
THUGS CRY
THUGS CRY 2
THUGS CRY 3
TRUST NO BITCH
TRUST NO BITCH 2
TRUST NO BITCH 3
TIL MY CASKET DROPS
RESTRAINING ORDER
RESTRAINING ORDER 2
IN LOVE WITH A CONVICT
LIFE OF A HOOD STAR
XMAS WITH AN ATL SHOOTER

www.ingramcontent.com/pod-product-compliance
Lightning Source LLC
LaVergne TN
LVHW010922110826
845149LV00013B/2448

* 9 7 8 1 9 7 1 7 7 0 2 1 5 *